Claudia

by BARBARA WALLACE

Illustrated by Ethel Gold

SCHOLASTIC BOOK SERVICES

NEW YORK • TORONTO • LONDON • AUCKLAND • SYDNEY

Copyright © 1969 by Barbara Wallace. This edition is published by Scholastic Book Services, a division of Scholastic Magazines, Inc., by arrangement with Follett Publishing Company.

1st printing .... November 1969

Printed in the U.S.A.

For Sheila, Jimmy, Lynda, and Michael,
without whom
this book might never have been.

One

A BRANCH of the large apple tree heaved up and down, its leaves making a wild, whishing sound, as Claudia began to bounce on it. The branch still shook when she dropped backward, her knees clamped around it. Then a special kind of waiting silence fell upon the tree as she hung there, head down and motionless. Her friend, Duffy, sharing the branch but sitting close to the tree trunk and clutching it firmly, watched her with admiration. The tree was in Duffy's backyard, which was two backyards and three climbing fences away from where Claudia lived.

From her upside-down position, Claudia reached out and picked a still-green apple from a limb in front of her. After inspecting it briefly for worm holes, she pulled herself up and began to nibble on it. Now she was ready to continue the conversation she and Duffy had been having.

"Well, I knew what I wanted to be when I was seven. That was four years ago. Here you are going on nine and you can't make up your mind! What's wrong with you, Duffy Booth?" Claudia watched Duffy look glumly at a black hole in *his* apple, about one quarter of an inch from where his teeth had sunk in.

Duffy sighed. "All right what did you decide when you were seven?"

"You remember," said Claudia.

"No, I don't," said Duffy.

"Then I'll give you a clue." Claudia raised a thin, sun-browned hand to her mouth and gave out a loud "Ah-ee-ah-ee-ah." Then she pounded her chest and said, "Me Tarzan, you Jane."

"It's the other way around," said Duffy. "Anyway, I have it. You want to star in a Tarzan movie."

"Wrong!"

"You want to become an ape?"

Claudia gave him a cold stare. "Well, I guess you give up. I'm going to be an animal doctor."

"That's a veterinarian," said Duffy. "And that was a pretty dumb clue, Claudia." Then, after thinking a moment, "Is that what Janice is going to be too . . . a veterinarian?"

"How should I know if she's going to be a veterinarian? I haven't seen her in two years."

"I guess you're glad she's coming back tomorrow," Duffy said rather wistfully.

"I guess so." Claudia shrugged and took a big bite from her apple. Actually, she was terribly excited about Janice Irby coming back. After all, Janice had once been her very best friend. That was before Janice and her family had gone away, and before Duffy had moved into the neighborhood and she had become friends with him. Of course, now she could hardly remember what Janice even looked like, but she did remember that Janice had a neat collection of Matchbox cars, as well as a large number of other neat collections. And she especially remembered that she and Janice had been almost like twins in the way they thought and acted, like two wild Indians, even though Janice was a year older than she was. Anyway, Claudia would have been something pretty strange if she hadn't been excited to know that the Irbys were returning and would soon be living in their same house again.

A loud clang-bang, clang-bang coming from the direction of Claudia's house interrupted her daydream.

"Is that for you?" Duffy asked. It was a pointless question, because they both knew that Claudia's family was the only one in the neighborhood who owned the old school hand bell that made that particular kind of noise. It was very definite.

"Claudia!" a voice rolled out, as if to dispel any doubts. It was the voice of Mrs. Harper, Claudia's mother.

"Coming!" Claudia yelled. Then she muttered, "I

7

don't understand how I ever thought that bell was a good idea. Now it makes me feel like a sheep or a cow."

"Well, you like animals," Duffy offered helpfully.

"Liking something doesn't mean you want to be it," Claudia said, exasperated.

With a groan, she threw down her apple core, grabbed the branch between her legs and did a back flip down to the next branch. She slid past the branch so quickly and on down to the ground that Duffy, following after, looked as if he thought she might have killed herself. When he got down himself, the slow way via the trunk, he found Claudia lying flat on the ground, arms and legs splayed out so she looked like a beached starfish. Her eyes were wide open and staring. Duffy poked her.

"Hey, Claudia, are you dead?" he whispered.

Claudia blinked at him, then drew her knees up to her face, hugging them and at the same time grinning through them at Duffy.

Duffy, relieved, giggled. "All curled up like that, you look like a dead bird, Claudia."

"Well, you know what *you* look like, Duffy? You look like something mighty fat. I can see from here that you are developing a very big stomach. Ha! With all those brains you have and with that big stomach, I think that's where you keep your brains, in your stomach! You're probably the only boy in the whole world running around with a stomach full of smart brains."

Looking pleased, Duffy puffed out his cheeks with air, stuck out his stomach and patted it proudly. Duffy's stomach, bulging tightly under his pale green, striped T-shirt, made him look as if he were pounding a ripe watermelon. Both Claudia and Duffy giggled wildly.

"Claudia!" The voice was more insistent and Claudia leaped lightly to her feet, heading for the fence. She stopped, however, when she realized that Duffy wasn't following her.

"Aren't you coming?" she asked.

"Do you think I should?"

"Why shouldn't you?"

"Your mother said she didn't want you playing with me so much. That's why I shouldn't," Duffy said. Still, he looked hopeful.

"Come on," Claudia said. "She's over that." She sounded as if her mother had finally recovered from a long-term childhood disease.

Duffy started toward her, his action suddenly putting into motion a stringy black mongrel who had been peacefully dozing in the sunshine and now realized almost too late that he was being left behind. This was Caesar's Ghost, Duffy's dog, who bounded after the children. As they hoisted themselves up and over the fence, he stood with paws up, stretched thin, with pleading eyes and an optimistic tail flailing the air joyously. He was rewarded only by a look of apology from Duffy.

Claudia and Duffy dropped over the fence into the

Hennessey yard and tore across with the Hennessey dog, Prince, barking at their heels. Prince was only eighteen inches long and one foot high, but he had somehow never found this out about himself and was, of all the dogs in the neighborhood, the fiercest and the noisiest. The children reached the opposite side of the yard safely and scaled the white rail fence into the Friedman yard where they found the Hennessey twins, Robin and Robby, playing "rope" with Leonie and Maurice Friedman.

"Rope" wasn't even a game, really, just something where everyone had a piece of string or rope and ran around dragging it on the ground making animal or cowboy noises. Claudia and Duffy both thought it was terribly dumb.

Anyway, as they trailed through the yard trying to look as if they weren't trespassing, the Friedmans' dog, Bagel, leaped over to them and nearly knocked them over with friendliness. Bagel was, like his neighbor dogs, a mongrel, but he was larger than the other two put together, mostly German shepherd, the Friedmans said. He had a long tongue which nearly always hung out drooling, and he loved everyone in the whole world violently, postmen, milkmen, burglars — everyone.

The children all stopped waving their ropes around and stood staring at Claudia and Duffy with round eyes.

"Your mother is calling you," Robin Hennessey said.

10

"Thanks a lot," said Claudia. She hadn't intended to sound snotty, but little kids were always telling you something that was already as plain as their noses. They probably didn't notice how she sounded anyway. She gave Bagel a self-conscious pat on the head and was rewarded by a slobbering kiss that reached from her chin to her hairline. Then she and Duffy climbed slowly and with dignity over the chain link fence that divided the Harper and Friedman houses.

Mrs. Harper was waiting for Claudia on their side service porch. She looked pretty and cool in a peppermint-pink-and-white striped cotton dress with a pink sweater thrown over her shoulders. Pink was her favorite color. She also looked ready to go out somewhere and Claudia had the uncomfortable feeling that she was supposed to know where.

When Mrs. Harper saw Duffy, she smiled at him in a rather absentminded way, almost as if he were, quite literally, Claudia's shadow — something of no consequence whatsoever. Claudia, however, she inspected sternly.

"Dear, I told you to stay close to the house. You knew," Claudia didn't of course, "that I was getting ready to go shopping. Where were you? Oh, never mind . . . you're here. Now please run in the house and get changed quickly. Just look at you!"

To satisfy her mother, Claudia eyed herself. She was wearing her last season's blue jeans, torn off at the knees to make a pair of summer shorts, and a boy's shirt with the sleeves rolled up. The shirt had be-

11

longed to her twenty-year-old brother when he was thirteen, and Claudia had worn it as a smock for finger painting in kindergarten. She had stubbornly refused to give it up, and the shirt had just as stubbornly refused to wear out. Although she was gradually growing into it, it still flapped comfortably around her like an old tent. Besides this, it was helpfully prestained with old kindergarten paints so that bark stains, grass stains, and the paw prints of dogs hardly showed at all.

At the moment, Claudia's feet looked the way they usually did in summer, bare and dusty, even though they had started out clean that morning. Claudia knew quite well that she looked grubby, but she gave her mother a bright, ignorant look. Mrs. Harper simply sighed and held open the door to the house.

Claudia suddenly remembered that Duffy was still standing there, quite possibly wondering why he had come. "Mother, can't Duffy go with us?"

"I'm sure Duffy's mother wouldn't want him coming with us," Mrs. Harper replied quickly.

"Oh, she might," said Duffy.

"But, Duffy dear, we're going downtown. To a department store!" Mrs. Harper opened her eyes at Duffy as if to suggest that a visit to a department store was something extraordinary and possibly not even proper for a young boy. It embarrassed Claudia to death.

"Mother," she said, "Duffy has been to a department store before."

"Claudia," said Mrs. Harper, "what I meant was that we are going to be buying some school clothes for you."

"That's just it!" Claudia burst out in a stricken voice. "School is starting next week!" This as a reason for Duffy going with them didn't make much sense at all, but Claudia made it sound like the last request of someone heading for her doom. She could see that her mother was weakening.

"Please!" she begged in a small, pleading voice.

"Oh, all right, though I should know better than to take the two of you together anywhere again," Mrs. Harper said finally, looking even more doubtful as the victorious and gleeful Claudia banged Duffy so hard on the back that he nearly fell over. "Duffy, run home and ask your mother if you can go with us. And be sure and tell her we're going downtown."

"Thank you, Mrs. Harper. Should I change my clothes, too?"

Mrs. Harper looked Duffy over critically. Duffy often managed to look respectable even in his play clothes. "No, Duffy," she said, "you can go the way you are. After all, you are a boy."

Now that was a strange thing to say, Claudia thought.

Two

CLAUDIA raced through the kitchen, stopping briefly at the refrigerator to pour herself a glass of milk. She almost never went anywhere without strengthening herself with a little something, on the theory that every time she left the house, even for five minutes, she might never see food again. Then she wiped her mouth off on her arm, tore out to the hall, and thumped up the steps two at a time.

Claudia's room was at the end of the hall. It was a tiny room, but exactly right for her. She could hardly believe now that the room had once been her brother David's, but it *had* been three years ago. Then, before he left for college, he had been given the spare room together with an entire set of new furniture, and Claudia had inherited his room. It had windows on two sides through which the sun poured, and from her desk now, she could look out one window and see Duffy's apple tree.

For as many years as she could remember, Claudia had shared a room with her older sister, Barbara, a room smothered in flowered chintz and pastel ribbons and haunted by two enormous, floppy, cloth dolls with staring blue eyes painted on flat white faces. Claudia had, with the considered help of her brother, labeled them Henbane and Hemlock. At last, in her own little room, she was finally relieved of the sight of those two near-witches.

Racing in, Claudia peeled off her shirt and shorts, dropping them on the floor where she stood. A second thought made her stoop to pick them up and hang them, folded, over a chair. Ever since she had moved into this room, she had done her best to be terribly neat — on her own. She liked things to be neat — pencils and erasers all lined up in a drawer, rocks and shells sorted into boxes and labeled — but sometimes this caring about her room was like being tied up in a straitjacket of neatness. It was just that she was so afraid someone would want to change things. She had begged to have everything left exactly as it was when David had the room, the old gray and black Indian rug, the plain oak bedstead, the chest of drawers, the small bookshelf which was just large enough to hold all of Claudia's favorite books, and the student

15

desk and chair. The top of the desk had been deeply engraved by a boy scout knife, a memorial to, in order, D. S. Harper, David S. Harper, D. Shelton Harper, and David Shelton Harper. Also plain David, Dave, and Harpy. Claudia adored the desk. In fact, she adored the whole room and wanted it to stay exactly the way it was forever.

Only two new things had been added. One was a plain blue denim bedspread with a white border (blue was Claudia's favorite color) and the second was a miniature carved Chinese chest which had its own little lock and key. It was on the bookcase. Something that might have been considered another addition to the room was Irma, the Harpers' fat gray cat, who had moved herself in along with Claudia and frequently formed, in a lumpy kind of way, an embroidery in the center of the bed. She rarely opened a sleepy eye even when Claudia flopped down beside her, and almost never treated anyone to the sound of her musical purr.

After a brief intermission to scratch Irma's ear, Claudia pulled on her blue jumper. She started to put on her sneakers without socks, but after another look, she decided she had better wear socks or her mother would send her back up to wash her feet. She didn't even bother to examine her face in a mirror, but raced back down the hall and down three steps. A change of mind made her climb back up and ride down via the bannister. Her mother was waiting for her in the living room. She studied Claudia with a practiced eye. "Well, I guess you'll have to do. Now where do you suppose Duffy is?"

A knock on the door answered the question and Duffy appeared, clothes changed and face scrubbed to a shiny pink. "You didn't have to go that far!" Claudia hissed at him.

They went out and climbed into the car, Claudia in the middle beside her mother and Duffy on the outside by the window. Mrs. Harper started to hum a little tune as soon as they were on their way. This was reassuring, and Claudia began to feel pleased and happy. But all at once, unfortunately, she became intensely aware of Duffy's stomach directly under her eye. It offered such a clear invitation that she stuck out her finger and gave it a quick jab. This brought Duffy to life with remarkable speed. He grinned wickedly at Claudia and dug her in the ribs. A scuffle followed.

"Now just a minute, you two," said Mrs. Harper. "If you don't settle down immediately, I'll stop this car in the first convenient place and there we'll sit until we have some order. I can see now that it was a mistake to agree to bring you two out together!"

They quieted down at once, but Claudia felt an overpowering urge to jab Duffy in the stomach again. To overcome it, she put her hands under herself and sat on them, hoping her mother was impressed with her goodness. Mrs. Harper was paying little attention to Claudia, however, because by now they had arrived at the store.

They went immediately to the girls' department, and about forty-five minutes and several arguments later, Claudia had acquired two plain white blouses, a red sweater, and a red-and-blue plaid skirt. Mrs. Harper looked exhausted.

"Pssst," whispered Duffy while she was charging the bill, "ask your mother if we can go to the toy department."

Claudia hadn't given much thought to the toy department. What was the use? She hated dolls and she wasn't allowed any of the things she considered interesting. Still, it would be fun to look with Duffy.

Mrs. Harper seemed almost relieved when Claudia asked if she and Duffy could visit the toy department while her mother did the rest of her shopping and, after promising perfect behavior, they boarded the escalator and rode sedately out of sight.

Of course, they no sooner reached the next escalator then they started playing games, running up five and down three steps, seeing if they could get almost to the top and then trying to get back down again. They might never have arrived at the toy department at all, except that at last they collided with a stout lady in a knit dress who was carrying an enormous rope satchel and wearing a large hat smothered in artificial flowers. The lady stared at them indignantly and it quieted them down.

In a moment, however, Claudia leaned over and whispered to Duffy, "Hey, you know what?"

"What?"

"That lady has a d-o-g in that bag!"

"How do you know?"

"I heard it when we bumped into her. Dogs aren't allowed in this store."

"What are you going to do about it?"

"Nothing, I guess," Claudia said with an indifferent shrug. At any rate, the lady got off on another floor, and they soon forgot about her in the joys of reaching the toy department.

The end-of-summer toy department can hardly compare with the beginning-of-Christmas toy department, but Claudia believed that she would never be so grown up as to stop having an indescribable feeling of joy from walking into a whole place filled with toys. She was beginning to notice, though, to her great disappointment, that the older she became, the fewer and fewer things she would find that she needed or even wanted. Still, she never remembered this when she first walked in, and that part of it always remained exciting.

She and Duffy stood a moment at the cashier's desk and then began strolling slowly down an aisle. They stopped in front of a display of sailboats.

A man, probably the floor manager, stood near the counter taking notes in an impressively large and black notebook. The notebook seemed almost to be growing from him, a natural outcropping of his tight black suit, and his pencil bore down harder on it when he saw Claudia fingering the sailboats. Claudia knew that he was watching them even though his head remained directed toward the notebook.

The boats were slick and beautiful, with smooth white hulls, shiny varnished decks, and seaworthy sails. Claudia spent so much time examining one that Duffy moved on without her. When she finally set the boat down, she saw that Duffy was over looking at the dolls. Sidling over to him, she whispered through clenched teeth, "What are you doing? Do you want to get contaminated!"

"I like dolls," Duffy said.

"You *what!*" screeched Claudia.

"I like dolls," said Duffy. "What's wrong with your ears?"

"You mean *dolls?* Any dolls? *Doll* dolls?" Claudia stared at him in complete disbelief.

"Well, not any dolls, Claudia. Mostly boy dolls. Like that boy doll I have with all the army and navy stuff. Then I have the troll. I don't know if you'd call that a doll."

"How come I've never seen those dolls?" asked Claudia, narrowing her eyes suspiciously.

"You have seen them," replied Duffy with a resigned sigh.

"Oh," said Claudia, remembering that she had. "Doesn't your mother mind you having dolls?"

"I guess not. She got them for me."

"I wonder if my mother would ever get me a football helmet or anything like that."

"I don't think so," said Duffy reasonably.

"No, she'd probably think it would make me grow up to be a football player. You know."

"I know," said Duffy.

Claudia picked up a rubber baby doll, gingerly lifting up the skirt of its dress to see what was underneath. "Urp! Lace! Come on, let's go."

They wandered off in the direction of a counter piled high with small boxes. Suddenly Claudia poked Duffy. "Hey, there's the lady with the dog!" She had seen the flowered hat sailing into the toy department.

"Do you think she still has it?" Duffy asked.

Claudia studied the toe of her sneaker, then leaned over and pulled off a piece of loose rubber. Rolling it between her fingers intently, she said, "We could find out."

Duffy rewarded this enterprising suggestion with a giggle.

"First," Claudia said, "I want to see what's in these." She opened one of the boxes on the counter and pulled out its contents, noticing at the same time that Black Notebook had moved over to a pillar by the counter and, while seeming to be busy with his pencil, was actually watching her.

"Water pistols!" Claudia said to Duffy in a loud

voice. "Boy! I wish we had some water! Boy! Squirt! Squirt!"

Duffy then opened a box and helped himself to a water pistol, aiming it at Claudia. Pointing the bright red plastic water pistols, they backed away from each other.

As Claudia rounded the end of the counter, she dipped down behind it. When she peered back out, she saw that Duffy had disappeared and that Black Notebook, his ears a bright pink, was frantically looking for them.

Claudia sank back down again and crawled on hands and knees in the opposite direction. She saw Duffy slinking two aisles down and went after him. "Squirt! Squirt!" she called out under her breath. Duffy caught sight of her and disappeared again. Claudia, still crawling, set out after him.

Suddenly, without having planned it at all, she found herself squatting in front of a familiar rope satchel. She put a hand up to her mouth to stifle a giggle and then, as she saw Duffy coming around the corner opposite her, pointed excitedly at the satchel. As the lady continued to amuse herself with a mechanical toy on the counter above them, Claudia nudged the satchel. In a way, she was only trying to see if a dog actually was inside, but somehow the satchel rolled over on its side, the top came unhinged, and a small Pekinese ambled out. He blinked at the sudden bright light, yawned an enormous yawn right in Claudia's face, and immediately thereafter began to sniff at her with a flat black nose set somewhere in the depths of his round, shrivelled-up balloon of a face.

Claudia leveled her water pistol at him. "Squirt! Squirt!"

"Werf! Werf!" replied the interested Pekinese.

Its owner, suddenly aware of the disaster at her feet, leaned over and tried desperately to stuff the dog back into the bag. He refused, however, to allow himself to be stuffed, and slipping from her grasp as if he had been greased, he went after Claudia.

Claudia jumped up and shouted to Duffy, "Quick, head him off at the pass!" Duffy, brandishing his water pistol in the air, chased after them.

Black Notebook, by now almost hysterical, found himself pursuing not only Claudia and Duffy, but a wildly yapping Pekinese and the dog's distraught owner as well. "Madam!" he called out. "Dogs are not allowed in the store!"

The lady stopped short and glared at him. "He wasn't in the store," she said, all dignity. "He was in my bag!" This magnificent display of logic seemed to leave Black Notebook speechless for a moment, although his lips nearly disappeared in a thin line of fury.

Claudia, who had been watching the scene with great interest, chose this moment to raise her water pistol, point it calmly at a head that was appearing at the top of the escalator and shout, "Squirt! Squirt!"

The head belonged to Mrs. Harper. Claudia gasped.

The look on Claudia's face must have alerted Black Notebook, because he approached Mrs. Harper immediately. Claudia and Duffy watched as a polite but strained conversation took place between them. Then, with the promise that the children would be dealt with at home, Mrs. Harper took Claudia and Duffy both by the hands, practically dragging them to the escalator. She said nothing on the way to the car, maintaining an angry silence. She said nothing on the way home, either, even though she didn't seem quite so angry.

But that night, Claudia was informed by both her parents that she would no longer be allowed to play with Duffy.

Three

THE NEXT MORNING, Claudia lay in bed for a long time, staring at the ceiling and trying to plan her day. The little clock by her bed told her that it was later than usual, but then she always managed to awaken later and later as the beginning of school drew nearer. Nevertheless, there were still a large number of hours in the day which had to be filled. To begin with, she would get in touch with Duffy. No, she now remembered, she could not get in touch with Duffy. Or at least she could not be seen doing it.

On several previous occasions, Claudia's mother and father had told her that she should not be playing with Duffy. It had somehow never stuck, but this time she was afraid they meant it. Claudia had tried to explain to them that the escapade in the department store was all her fault. Nobody was blaming Duffy, they said, but they felt that if Duffy hadn't been along, the whole thing would never have happened. This was probably true, and there was no use in arguing the point. It was always easier for Claudia to get into trouble with Duffy offering his loyal support.

It was a good thing that Janice was coming back that day. With that happy thought, Claudia gave herself a small hug of excitement, then threw back her covers and leaped out of bed. Although she still had a few hours to fill before Janice's arrival, she decided that she would go ahead and put on her good shorts and a striped knit shirt. Then she decided that she might as well put on her sneakers, since with Duffy's yard out of bounds, there was no telling where she would go or what she might do. After that, she raced to the kitchen with such speed that she arrived breathless.

"What's the big rush?" asked Barbara, still in bathrobe and hair curlers.

"I'm late," replied Claudia, flopping down at the table.

"Late for what, dear?" asked her mother.

"Just late," said Claudia.

Mr. Harper put down the morning paper. "I wish I could see all this display of energy on a school morning."

"She probably has a date with Duffy," Barbara said with a self-righteous sniff.

"No, dear," Mrs. Harper said. "Claudia is not going to be playing with Duffy anymore."

Barbara's eyebrows raced up her forehead. "Well, that's a nice surprise."

"What's wrong with Duffy?" said Claudia, glaring at her sister.

"Nothing's wrong with Duffy," Mr. Harper interrupted. "Duffy is quite a gentleman, in fact."

"What's wrong," Barbara went on, ignoring her father, "is that you are an eleven-year-old girl and Duffy is an eight-year-old boy. That's what's wrong."

"He's almost nine!" Claudia shrieked. "Anyway, when did you stop liking boys?"

"Girls! Girls!" Mrs. Harper exclaimed. She pulled a saucepan of boiling water from the stove and ran cold water into it. They all watched her as she dipped out the boiled eggs, sliced each one with a quick, hard tap of the knife, and scooped them out into tea cups. "Well, dear," she said to Claudia after the cups had been set out, "isn't it nice that Janice is due back today?"

Claudia knew that her mother was only trying to change the subject, but somehow the remark made her cross. It sounded as if Janice was replacing Duffy. She was excited herself about Janice returning, but she never would have thought of giving up playing with Duffy to play with Janice. They were two separate friends.

Claudia stuffed her mouth with the last of her toast and nearly choked to death on her orange juice as she tried to eat and talk and rise from the table all at the same time. "Yes, it is. I guess I don't want any egg. Excuse me please," she mumbled as she started for the back door.

Barbara threw a parting comment at her. "I don't expect that Janice will even look at Claudia anymore."

Claudia stopped short with her hand on the door handle. "Why not?"

"Oh, I just don't think she will. After all, she's been away two years. *She's* probably changed and grown up a little."

Claudia didn't wait to hear any more and slammed out the door, standing on the back porch a moment to think over what Barbara had said. Not that it was worth thinking over. What would Janice have to grow up about? Anyway, what if she had? Claudia had grown up too. At least she was taller. All that had probably happened to Janice was that she had grown an inch or two. Claudia hoped that she hadn't grown so much that they couldn't trade sweatshirts the way they once did.

At this point, Claudia realized that she didn't have a single thing planned to do. It was much too early to go over and see if Mrs. Irby and Janice had arrived. The moving van and Mr. Irby had arrived almost simultaneously two days before and Claudia, wandering by, had found out that Janice and her mother were visiting relatives in New York but would be home today, probably in the afternoon.

Claudia took a quick glance at her kitchen window and then with the kind of side step a crab uses, which makes him look as if he doesn't want to go in the direction he is taking, Claudia sidled off toward Duffy's house.

Leonie and Maurice Friedman were out in front of their house taking turns trying to jump rope with a piece of laundry line that was too short even for Maurice. "Why don't you get a longer rope?" Claudia said. Leonie smiled at her but went right on trying to jump over the too-short piece of line. Claudia shrugged her shoulders and went on. She liked Leonie a lot but the rope business was sometimes too much for her.

After quickly passing the Hennessey house, Claudia ducked into the Booths' driveway and ran up to the fence. Duffy's leg was, as Claudia had hoped, hanging down from the tree.

"Psssst!" she called out.

A face appeared through the branches. "Hey! Come on up!"

"I can't. I can't play with you anymore."

"Again?"

"That's right," said Claudia, still not making any attempt to leave.

Duffy left the tree, arriving at the fence with Caesar's Ghost at his heels. "I figured this would happen," he said, leaning over the fence. "You know . . . after yesterday."

"I know," said Claudia. "But it wasn't even your fault."

"That doesn't matter. As my father would say, it's the principle of the thing."

"What does that mean?" Claudia asked.

"I'm not sure. All I know is it doesn't have anything to do with facts." A deep silence followed this significant piece of information. "What did they say?" Duffy continued. "I guess they don't like me very well."

"It's not that, Duffy. They like you all right. My mother once said you were precocious."

"That's not too good," Duffy said.

"Why not?"

"Well, when someone says you're precocious, it means that they think your parents think you're a genius, but they personally think you're a brat." Duffy said this quite matter-of-factly.

"That's not what my family thinks. Honest."

"You mean they don't think I stink?"

"I said they like you. My dad even says you're a gentleman. It's just that they don't like us playing together because I'm eleven and you're only going on nine. Or something like that."

"That's never going to change," said Duffy gloomily. After this, there was another silence.

"You want to come with me?" Claudia asked suddenly, so suddenly, in fact, that she even took herself by surprise.

"I thought we weren't supposed to play together."

"I didn't say we were going to play. I'm just going someplace. Do you want to come or not?"

Without replying, and with no further questions, Duffy climbed over the fence and stood beside Claudia, ready to go.

What happened was that Claudia remembered it was Friday. On Fridays she always went to "this place." She had never told Duffy about it before. She had never told anyone about it before because there didn't seem to be any reason for telling anyone. There was not much reason now except that Duffy's chin was practically dragging the ground. Anyway, what Claudia had said was right — this was not playing. What they would be doing was not playing, so it would be all right.

They trudged along in silence for a while, not even bothering to avoid the cracks in the pavement. Finally, Duffy decided to say something. "Is that why you're wearing shoes? Because of the place you're going?"

"No, it isn't," Claudia said abruptly. She just didn't feel like having to explain shoes, for heaven's sake. After all, Duffy wasn't explaining *his* shoes. (Claudia knew she was being unreasonable. In the first place, she hadn't asked him about his shoes, and in the second place she already knew the answer. Duffy was allergic to bee stings and his mother made him wear shoes all the time.)

They covered two blocks doing nothing more exciting than hobbling along with one foot in the gutter and the other on the sidewalk. Then, when they arrived at a low, crumbling brick wall, they scrambled on and walked along it with arms outstretched, balancing precariously. When they arrived at the stone building which was the parish house of the Presbyterian church next to it, they slipped into the entry for a drink of water, not because either of them was thirsty, but just because they had once discovered a drinking fountain there. After that, instead of returning to the sidewalk, they scaled the hill that ran across the back of the church parking lot and went over the railroad track, half sliding, half running down the other side. They ended up sitting down, thereby acquiring streaks of black grease across their bottoms.

"I didn't know we were going this far away," Duffy said. "I don't think I'm allowed. Maybe I should call home when we get there."

"This place doesn't have a telephone," said Claudia. "Anyway, we won't be gone long."

They had left the residential section and had reached a block of shops. Claudia headed for the variety store. "Hey, is this all you're going to do? They *have* a telephone here," Duffy said.

"Well, this isn't really the place we're going. Anyway, do you have a dime?" Claudia asked.

"Nope," replied Duffy, following her in.

Claudia headed for the lunch counter, climbed onto a stool, and leaned on the counter, waiting. The counter girl, who was tiny and pale and had dark smudges under her eyes even at that hour of the day, finished serving someone coffee and a doughnut and came toward her. She reached into her apron pocket and pulled out a brown envelope, which she handed to Claudia.

A tense, worried look left the girl's eyes and she smiled, a sudden, warm smile. "Thanks, honey. And look, would you tell Momma they have a special on hamburger at Bob's. Say, is this your little friend?"

Claudia nodded, but without looking at Duffy.

"He's a nice little boy, honey. Hey, tell you what . . . let me get you something . . . on the house. What'll it be?"

"Well . . ." Claudia hesitated.

"Aw, come on!"

Duffy picked up the menu immediately and began to read it. "I'll have a banana spl . . ." Claudia gave him a sharp dig in the ribs.

"We'll both have a small Coke, Rosa," she said.

"You sure that's all?"

"Sure," said Claudia with another left to Duffy's ribs.

"Okay, honey." The girl, Rosa, gave them their Cokes and started rinsing dishes.

"Look, Duffy," Claudia hissed, "when somebody asks to buy you something, you don't order the most expensive thing on the menu. See? Especially when they're poor."

"Okay," said Duffy agreeably.

They sucked slowly on their Cokes, competing to

see who could make the loudest noises as they drained the last drops at the bottom of their glasses. Then, even though it made their teeth ache and grow numb, they chewed on the chipped ice until that, too, was all gone.

"I guess we'll go now, Rosa," Claudia said, getting up to leave and giving Duffy's T-shirt a warning pull. "Thanks a lot for the Cokes."

"Yes, thank you," Duffy added.

"That's nothing. Anyway, you're a doll. You know, she's a doll," Rosa said, the last addressed to Duffy. Duffy merely stared while Claudia turned pink. She brushed some hair nervously away from her forehead and turned to go.

"See you later, Rosa. Oh, and look, next week school starts so I can't come until afternoon . . . okay?"

"That's fine, honey."

"Well, 'bye then. Come on, Duffy." Claudia held on to a piece of Duffy's shirt and steered him toward the door.

"What was that all about?" Duffy asked, once they were outside.

"Nothing much. I just take her pay home to her mother and her kids."

Duffy puffed his cheeks out with air. "All that money?"

"It's not all that money," said Claudia. "She doesn't make all that money."

"How come you do it?" Duffy asked.

Claudia shrugged. "The first time it was an accident.

34

I went in for a soda and she asked me if I would do her a favor and run home with a message because they don't have a telephone. She wanted to give me a dime for it."

"A dime? Did you take it?"

"Of course not, dumbbell!" Claudia lapsed into silence, walking along kicking at the sidewalk with the toes of her sneakers.

"Well?" said Duffy.

"Well what?"

"Well what about the rest of it?"

"Nothing much. It was Friday that day . . . after school. I don't know . . . I just used to go in on Fridays and she started asking me to take this money home. They run out of money Thursday night, I guess, and Rosa's mother needs her pay to buy groceries. So I go in every Friday and take it to her." Claudia signaled the end of the explanation by starting to whistle.

They crossed the street and went down another two blocks, turning in at a run-down frame house that sat between a boarded-up electrical repair shop and another ragged frame house. Two small children sat on the front steps of the house they approached. When they saw Claudia and Duffy, they jumped up and ran in the house. The screen door was still trembling on its hinges when Claudia went up and banged on it.

"Ah! Ah!" a woman's voice cried out.

"What does that mean?" Duffy asked. He looked a little scared.

"It just means to come in," Claudia said. "She doesn't speak much English."

They walked into a small, searingly hot room filled with so much furniture it seemed to have breathed up all the air around it. The room was suffocating. Claudia felt her face breaking out wet all over.

The yellow blinds were half pulled down, making it difficult at first to see if anyone was in the room, but then they saw that another child about the size of a small goblin in a dirty undershirt was sitting on the back of the large, flat, green frieze couch. He was sucking his thumb and staring at them

"Where is she?" whispered Duffy.

"Come on," Claudia said, pulling him by the hand. Their hands already felt sticky when they touched.

They walked into what seemed to be just an extension of the living room, which contained one table and six unmatched chairs, and then on through an open door into the kitchen. Duffy remained standing in the doorway but Claudia marched right in.

An ancient gas stove occupied the space against the wall farthest to the right of the door, and the two small children who had been on the outside steps were now standing by its legs. They were pulling on the long black skirt of a woman who stood in front of the stove, holding a baby in one arm and using the other to poke at something in a very large pot on the stove. The water in the pot was sending off throaty rumbles and breathing forth choking clouds of steam. The woman was looking toward the door and when she saw Claudia, her heavy-jowled, wrinkled face, shiny with sweat, broke into a glorious smile, exposing a mouth decorated with five old teeth that looked more like hooks than anything else.

"Claude! Claude!"

"Hi, Mrs. Olivetti!" said Claudia, holding up the brown envelope. "Here . . . is . . . money. *Money!*" She was using the loud voice one uses when speaking to foreigners, as if they were all deaf.

The smile never left Mrs. Olivetti's face and she continued to stir the brew on the stove. It was as if she actually *were* deaf. Then she nodded her head toward Duffy. "Your friend?"

"He's . . . Duffy Booth!" shouted Claudia.

"Ah, Duffy! Nice!" said Mrs. Olivetti. She kept on smiling and stirring.

"Mrs. Olivetti," said Claudia firmly, "here . . . is . . . your . . . money."

"Ah . . . *money!*" exclaimed Mrs. Olivetti, the light of understanding finally arriving on her face.

Claudia set the envelope down on the linoleum counter. "Rosa says . . . sale . . . on . . . hamburger . . . at Bob's."

"Ah!" said Mrs. Olivetti. She turned the flame off on the stove, walked over and sat the baby in an old grocery cart that seemed to pass as a baby carriage, undid her apron, and picked up the envelope. "I go . . . I go," she said. Then, pointing at the baby and the children (all three of them were now in the kitchen), "You watch. I come right back."

"Okay, Mrs. Olivetti," Claudia said, walking over to the stove and poking down whatever it was in the pot with the large spoon still sitting in it.

Mrs. Olivetti beamed at her, beamed even more broadly at Duffy and nodded her head at him, then turned and left through the back door. Duffy just stood gaping, first at the departing back of Mrs. Olivetti and then at Claudia.

"What do we do now?" he asked, approaching the stove.

"Wait until she gets back."

Duffy looked into the pot and saw what appeared to be a lot of white rags swimming in a kind of gray soup. "What's that?"

"It's for the baby."

"They're going to feed the baby *that!*"

"Look, Duffy, where are your brains? These are the baby's pants . . . diapers." Claudia dished up some of the gray liquid in the spoon and let it trickle back out.

"Oh," said Duffy, looking impressed.

The three small children stood gazing as Claudia continued to stir the rags. Finally, one of them opened a counter drawer and rummaged around in it, bringing out two thin, cardboard-covered books which looked as if mice had been nesting on them. The edges were chewed and dirty. He took the books to Claudia, pulled on the hem of her shorts, and handed the books to her. Claudia took the books from him and then sat herself down in the one available kitchen chair. The three children sat on the floor around her.

"What are you going to do now?" Duffy asked.

"Read to them," said Claudia. "You might as well make yourself comfortable." She pointed grandly to the floor and Duffy squatted down crosslegged on a ragged cotton rug in front of the sink.

Claudia began to read. The story was something about a new puppy and Duffy looked bored. He became more interested when the baby started to make restless noises in the grocery cart, but Claudia simply stretched out one hand, took hold of one end of the cart, and began to push it gently back and forth. The baby began to chew on its finger and soon fell asleep.

When Claudia had finished the first book, she read the second. "Now what are you going to do?" asked Duffy, when she had finished that one too.

"Read them again."

"Don't they have any more books?"

"Nope," said Claudia, starting again to read about the new puppy.

The three children remained just as interested in the second reading, and the third and the fourth, as they had been in the first. Claudia, however, began casting desperate glances at the door. She was rewarded finally by the sight of a dripping Mrs. Olivetti heaving through it with a grocery sack.

"We have . . . to . . . go . . . Mrs. Olivetti!" Claudia shouted at her.

"Ah . . . have drink . . . have drink!" Mrs. Olivetti shouted back. She set down the sack and pulled out of it a package of Kool-aid, waving it at the children.

"Thank you . . . no. We . . . have . . . to . . . go," Claudia insisted. Mrs. Olivetti and the small children all beamed at her (it seemed the first time the children had done anything but stare) and walked with Duffy and Claudia to the front door.

For a whole block, Claudia marched along in silence, with Duffy having to two-step to keep up with her. Then at last she slowed down and they moved along at their usual dawdling pace. Duffy was thinking deeply.

"Don't they have a father?" he asked.

"I guess so," replied Claudia.

"What does he do?"

"I don't know. Drives a truck or something."

"Have you ever seen him?"

"Nope."

"Oh," said Duffy. Then, "Claudia?"

"Yep?"

"If you go again, could I go with you?"

"Maybe."

By mutual, and silent, consent, they drifted into the church parish hall for a drink of water from the fountain.

"Duffy?" said Claudia on their way out.

"What?"

"You had better not tell anyone about it. Not your mother. Not anyone."

"Okay."

"Cross your heart and hope to die?"

"Sure," Duffy said. He crossed his heart and then put out his hand. Claudia took it and shook it solemnly.

Then, running, they headed for home. About a block from their houses, they separated and went by two different routes so they would not be seen arriving together.

Four

WHEN CLAUDIA walked into her kitchen, she saw that her mother was also standing at the stove, stirring something that bubbled a creamy white in the saucepan, except that her mother looked cool and neat in white Bermuda shorts and a pink shirt, with her hair held back by a pink scarf. The whole kitchen, in fact, looked suddenly cool and neat to Claudia. And instead of drowning in the steam of cooking laundry, it was drifting in the scent of something lightly tinged with vanilla.

"Where have you been?" asked Mrs. Harper, peering into the saucepan as if she were addressing its contents.

"Out," Claudia said.

"You weren't playing with Duffy, were you?" her mother asked.

"What's for lunch?" replied Claudia, opening the refrigerator door and studying the shelves carefully. She found, however, that all she was doing was staring into the blank faces of seven extra-large eggs.

"Shut the refrigerator door, please . . . and I repeat, you weren't playing with Duffy, were you?"

"Nope," said Claudia. "I wasn't *playing* with anyone." She shut the refrigerator door with studious care.

"Well, Mrs. Booth telephoned here to find out where Duffy was. It seems that he disappeared without saying anything." Mrs. Harper shot a quick look at Claudia and then began to shift some plates in the cupboard.

"He'll be back," said Claudia. She allowed a respectful moment of silence for the departed Duffy to pass. "What's for lunch?"

"We're not out of peanut butter, if that's what you meant. And by the way, I almost forgot, Janice telephoned."

"Janice!" Claudia shrieked, leaping out of her chair. "Why didn't you say so?"

"I just did," replied Mrs. Harper.

"What did you tell her? What did you tell her?"

"I told her you'd probably be over as soon as you had returned to the fold *and* had finished your lunch," said Mrs. Harper pointedly.

Claudia drummed impatiently on the table while

her mother made her peanut-butter sandwich and then when it was placed before her, stuffed it into her mouth in great choking bites. She ordinarily nibbled around the edges, saving one round, crust-free bite until last, but she was presently in too big a hurry to stand on this formality.

As she raced out the back door, her mother called after her, "Aren't you going to change? Are you going to wear those filthy sneakers? And did you know you have a grease stain all over the rear end of your shorts?"

"Janice won't mind!" Claudia yelled back, disappearing from the sight of her house as rapidly as possible so her mother would have no chance to insist on anything.

Claudia raced most of the way, slowing down once when she happened to remember what Barbara had said about Janice changing. So what? Claudia said to herself. She would have had to change a little in two years unless she was a moron or something. The only thing that worried her was the stationery Janice had used to write that she was coming back. The letter itself was the polite kind your parents make you write, but that was all right because Claudia hated to write, too. It was the stationery that bothered her, pale blue with a bunch of drippy roses in the corner. Janice used to have some white paper with pictures of dogs on it. Still, Claudia reasoned, some dumb aunt had probably given her the blue stuff. She immediately dismissed the whole matter from her mind.

The door to the Irby house was wide open, but Claudia knocked anyway. She waited awhile and when no one came, she walked into the hall. It was cluttered with boxes and things recently unpacked from a moving van, but, looking around, Claudia saw that a large, gilt-framed mirror had already been hung on the wall. She passed the time by examining herself in it, concluding at last that she should at least have combed her hair before coming over, and washed off the grease stain that ran across the bridge of her nose. She tried rubbing the stain and only succeeded in smearing it around.

Suddenly, reflected in the mirror, Claudia saw a strange girl coming down the stairs behind her. She whirled around.

"Oh, I thought I heard someone down here," the girl said. "Claudia?"

Holy tomato, Claudia thought, this was Janice! She had the uncomfortable feeling that Janice was staring at the smudge on her nose.

"Hi," Claudia said limply.

"Hi," Janice returned with an equal lack of enthusiasm.

"My mother said you telephoned."

"Oh, yes, I did," Janice said. She sounded as if she had really forgotten all about it. "I'm still unpacking.

Come on up to my room." She turned and started back up the stairs.

Claudia followed, wondering how much longer they would go on acting stiff as a couple of fence posts. Perhaps only until they got into Janice's room and started playing with her Matchbox cars the way they used to. Janice once had the best collection in the whole neighborhood. Still, Claudia began to have the queer feeling that it wouldn't be so easy, and this was because of the way Janice was going up the stairs. She was taking mincing little steps and her back end was swaying back and forth in a kind of wiggle. Claudia was horrified, but fascinated too, wondering if *she* looked the same way from behind. She certainly hoped not!

Janice's room didn't look the same as it once had, either. She had the same room she'd had when the Irbys were there before, but you could hardly recognize it. All the old, dog-eared stuffed animals were gone, or at least they were not in sight. The battered microscope, the rock collection — everything even remotely interesting — was gone. The furniture had all been painted a pale green, and there was a lot of lavender every place you looked — the curtains thrown over the rods ready to be hung, the bedspreads, even something draped around a dressing table. It was all pretty sickening.

The beds were still covered with Janice's clothes ready to be put away. As the girls walked in, something in the middle of a pile of sweaters moved, stood up, and yawned. The thing was gray and about the size of a skein of wool.

"Oh, a dog!" exclaimed Claudia. "May I hold it?"

Janice leaped for the small animal and picked it up, cradling it in her arms. She started nuzzling the dog's face, ignoring Claudia's request entirely.

Claudia tried another approach. "What kind is it?" she asked, even though she knew quite well what kind it was.

"Toy poodle," Janice replied with an indifferent shrug and a look on her face suggesting that Claudia probably couldn't even tell time.

This didn't stop Claudia. "What's its name?" she asked.

"She has a lot of names. All pedigreed dogs do. I call her La Petite."

She continued nuzzling the dog and making cooing sounds to it while Claudia sat and looked on. Claudia knew by now that something had happened to Janice. She wasn't even trying. She didn't even care.

"I'm going to be a veterinarian," Claudia blurted out, knowing as soon as she had said the words that she really sounded stupid.

"Oh, really? How nice," Janice murmured, not even looking at her. There was continued silence.

"Could I get you something to drink?" Janice asked finally.

"No, thanks," Claudia said and then, overwhelmed

by the fact that Janice had actually said something on her own, she continued with, "Do you still have those neat Matchbox cars, Janice?"

Janice looked into her dog's face, smiling as if she and the poodle shared a secret. "Dear me, no. I forgot I ever had them. I don't know where they are, really. I think Mother gave them away to the Salvation Army or something."

Claudia couldn't decide whether she felt uncomfortable or just disgusted. The visit was a great big nothing. Why had Janice even bothered to telephone her? She was clearly not very happy about Claudia's being there. This was a fine turn of events — she wasn't allowed to play with Duffy and Janice didn't want to play with her. Ha! Ha! Ha! Claudia decided there was no point in staying around any longer so she stood up to go. She was just opening her mouth to announce her departure, when the doorbell rang.

Without excusing herself, Janice tore out of the room, still holding her dog, and leaving Claudia standing there not knowing quite what to do with herself. Claudia heard Janice squeal with delight as she welcomed someone at the door, this followed by loud whispers and giggles and, finally, the sound of footsteps on the stairs. Then Janice entered the room with another girl. Their arms were twined around each other and they looked terribly chummy. The other girl (Claudia knew her immediately) was Polly McKisson. The pill.

At least that was the way Claudia and Janice had always described her in the past. She had always been a real sissy, in their estimation, one who never seemed to do much but run around sticking out her tongue at people. She would look at you for an uncomfortably long time through her pale, washed-out blue eyes, and then end up sticking out her tongue at you, anyway, no matter what you had said. She was not merely a pill, she was a pill and a half. She didn't look much different now except that Claudia was suspicious that she might be wearing lipstick.

"You remember Polly, don't you?" Janice asked, smirking.

"Oh, sure," replied Claudia. "Hi!"

"Hello, Claudia," said Polly, putting her tongue up to the front of her teeth and then quickly drawing it in again. "I guess I haven't seen you since I got back from Boston." She smiled archly at Janice.

"Boston!" exclaimed Claudia, almost shrieking. "What were you doing in Boston?"

"I spent last summer there with my *ah*nt," said Polly.

"Your what?" boomed Claudia.

"My *ah*nt," repeated Polly, drawing out the ah for Claudia's benefit.

So that was it, thought Claudia. Polly had spent the summer with her *ah*nt (ha!) in Boston and had somehow reached Janice. She wondered if in order to be friends with Janice again she would have to take Polly in a package deal. It was a purely poisonous thought.

Then she realized that this was probably not a decision she would have to make as the girls clearly didn't want her around. She was about as useful there as a loose tooth.

The silence in the room became increasingly pointed. Janice and Polly were sitting close together on a bed and Polly kept leaning over and petting the dog. Every so often Claudia saw the glances of the two girls meet and their eyebrows flick upward. Not only that, Claudia now noticed something that should have been evident when the two girls appeared in the doorway together, and that was that they were wearing matching jersey shirts and little sandals with straw flowers across the arch. She became painfully aware of her sneakers, her grease-stained shorts, and particularly the grease smudge across her nose.

"Well, it's been nice seeing you, Janice," she said suddenly.

"Oh, must you go," said Janice with another long look at Polly.

"I guess so," Claudia said. "Nice to have seen you again, Polly."

Polly just stared at her with her pale blue eyes, and Claudia saw the tip of her tongue appear and disappear again. Claudia found herself backing up to the door to hide the grease stain on her shorts.

"I'll see you to the door," Janice volunteered half-heartedly.

"That's okay. I can find it," Claudia said. She was simply dying to stick out her tongue at Polly, but chose instead to make a dignified exit. All her dignity exploded in her face, though, when, going down the stairs, she heard stifled giggles in the room behind her.

She ran blindly toward the front door, afraid that she was going to make a dope of herself and cry, but wondering at the same time why anyone would want to cry over two such horsey petunias.

She was startled and not at all happy to see Mrs. Irby, Janice's mother, puffing through the door from the living room with her round little arms piled high with bed linens. She dropped them on a cardboard carton with a thump when she saw Claudia. After two years, Claudia had almost forgotten, too, how Mrs. Irby looked.

She was a small person about four sofa pillows tall and three around — fat sofa pillows. She usually wore on her face one of only two expressions. The first was the one where she looked at the world through bland, melting eyes, which gave you the feeling that she might at any moment burst into a moo. And the second was where little wrinkles appeared between her eyebrows, making her look either worried or in mild pain. It was this second expression she was using on Claudia.

"Oh dear, I didn't even know you'd come, Claudia dear. Are you leaving already?"

"Yes, Mrs. Irby," Claudia replied.

"Is there . . . is there . . . someone else up there with Janice?"

"Polly McKisson," said Claudia.

"Oh, dear," said Mrs. Irby. "Well, I guess I shouldn't have had her call . . . that is . . . well, never mind. Do say hello to your mother, dear."

"Yes, I will. Thank you. Good-bye, Mrs. Irby."

Claudia tried to walk slowly away from the house, knowing that Janice and Polly might be watching from the window, but as soon as she had rounded the block, she started to run. She was running so fast that the tears on her face flew off into the hot, summer air.

Five

"I HATE THEM!" Claudia hunched down, dug her elbows into her knees and her fists into her chin, and stared darkly ahead.

"You said that before," Duffy told her from a position on a branch nearby. It was Sunday, and Claudia and Duffy were sitting in Duffy's apple tree.

"Well, I'll say it again and again. I hate them! I hate them!"

"Why?" Duffy asked.

"None of your business, Duffy. I just hate them, that's all."

"What are you going to do about it?" asked Duffy as he carefully split an apple leaf down the center vein.

Claudia scowled, remaining silent for a moment. "Who said I was going to do *any*thing about it?"

"Well, aren't you?"

"Maybe."

"Like what?" asked Duffy, dissecting another leaf.

Claudia looked at him sideways, then lowered her eyelids. "I'm declaring war!" she said softly.

"War!" yelped Duffy. "How can you do that?"

"Keep your voice down!" Claudia hissed. "Do you want your mother to find me?"

"That's okay," said Duffy. "She doesn't care if we play together."

"Yes, but she might mention it to my mother and she does care."

This seemed to cover the subject of Claudia's mother and no further comments were needed about it. There was another silence.

"Okay, you're going to declare war," Duffy said at last. "How can you have a war if you don't have an army?"

"I've got an army," Claudia said with disgust. "You, for one thing."

"Claudia, how can we go to war together when we're not even allowed to play together?" Duffy said patiently.

"Look, Duffy, do I have to explain everything? This is going to be a private war. You don't think I'm going around advertising it, do you? We'll just have the war when no one's looking."

"Even the enemy?" asked Duffy.

"Duffy, look, we are just going to spy on them. Besides, if that dumb Janice and that dumb Polly knew I was having a war against them, they'd just tell my family and phhhht . . . no more war."

"Okay," said Duffy. "What am I going to be in your army, Claudia?"

"A private, I guess."

"That's not very much."

"Well, I'm going to be an officer and you can't have a whole army with just two officers. So I'll be a general and you'll be the private."

"That's a pretty skinny army," Duffy said.

"Look, Duffy, what do you want me to do about it? Put up posters and get recruits?"

Duffy still looked glum.

"Hey, I've got it!" exclaimed Claudia, nearly tumbling off her branch in excitement. "We *will* get recruits! We'll have a *real* army!"

"What kind of recruits?" Duffy asked.

"We'll get Leonie and Maurice. Then we'll get Robin and Robby."

Duffy sighed. "Claudia, they are just *babies*."

"Leonie's almost as old as you are. Besides, why would you want older kids, anyway? This way you can get promoted."

"Oh, okay," Duffy agreed, smiling.

"And listen, Duffy," Claudia continued. She had lowered her voice to a mysterious and almost inaudible whisper. "We're going to need swords, helmets, stuff like that." They both knew that Duffy was the only one who had that kind of equipment.

"Okay," he said again.

"Duffy, why don't you go get whatever you can carry and I'll go get recruits."

"What if they don't want to be recruits?" Duffy asked.

"Look, Duffy," said Claudia, "they will want to be recruits." Her tone of voice told Duffy that they would either join up or get drafted. "Also," she said, "you ought to bring a . . . a pledge."

"What's that?"

"This is a *secret* army," Claudia said pointedly. "We have to have a pledge to keep it a secret."

"You mean like drawing blood?"

"Something like that, only not exactly. They wouldn't do anything like drawing blood."

"What should I bring, Claudia?"

"Something important. Really important."

"Okay," Duffy said, and started to climb down from the tree.

"Hey, wait a minute," Claudia whispered. "We can't be seen leaving this tree together. Look, I'll go first. Then you get the stuff and meet us on the Friedmans' front lawn."

"But we'll be seen there, won't we?" asked Duffy.

"It won't matter there. No one said I couldn't play with them." Claudia dropped down from the tree and ran to the fence, climbing over it quickly. Caesar's Ghost barked at her a few times through the fence and then ran back under the tree and sat down, looking impatiently up into the branches.

Leonie and Maurice Friedman and Robin and Robby Hennessey were all flat on their stomachs on the ground when Claudia arrived at the Friedmans' front lawn. They were peering intently at something either on or in the grass and none of them saw Claudia. Maurice finally looked up, saw her standing over them and, with his dark eyes round and serious, said, "I found a caterpillar."

"What kind?" Claudia asked.

"A black and yellow one," Leonie said.

"It squishes when it walks," Robin added, blinking her wide blue eyes at Claudia.

"It has hairs. It has hairs all over," announced Robby, rubbing his own hairless, pink cheeks.

"I found it," Maurice said again.

"Where is it? I don't see anything," Claudia said, peering down between them.

Maurice clenched a fist and pounded it on the ground. "It's there. It's right there where I put it."

Leonie reached out and pulled his fist back. "Maurice! You killed it! You killed it to death!"

"No, I didn't! It's right there," Maurice said, this time pointing. "Look, I'll show you." He pulled back several blades of grass and with them the squashed remains of a yellow and black caterpillar. His eyes filled with tears and his lips began to quiver as the three others looked at him accusingly.

"I found it," he said helplessly.

"Maurice, there's no use finding something if you're going to go and kill it right away," his sister told him.

"I didn't mean to," he said, tears rolling down his cheeks. "I l-l-l-loved it!"

"Hey, I've got a good idea," Claudia burst in. "Let's play army."

The four children looked at her blankly.

"Look," Claudia continued a little desperately, "we'll have a war. It'll be a secret war."

"I like secrets," Robin said.

Leonie appeared puzzled. "Who will we have a war against?"

"Oh, I'll tell you about that later," Claudia replied with a breezy wave of her arm. "That's . . . that's part of the secret."

"I guess I'd like to," Leonie said.

Robby began to jump up and down. "I want to be in the army, too!"

"We'll all be in the army," Claudia said importantly.

Maurice kept staring at the ground where his dead caterpillar lay, and finally he threw his face into his arms and sobbed, "I don't want to play army!"

"Hey, look, Maurice," Claudia said. "Look what we'll do. We'll call our army the caterpillar army. The caterpillar will be our dead hero . . . see? And the first thing we'll do is have this big funeral . . . a military funeral. And then ever after that, when someone in the army does something brave, they'll get a yellow and black medal in honor of this dead caterpillar hero. Would you like that, Maurice?"

Everyone looked at Maurice as he stared first at the caterpillar and then at Claudia, the tears sparkling on his long, dark eyelashes. Suddenly he grinned. "Can I have a medal for finding him?" he asked.

"Sure," said Claudia. "You can have two."

"Here comes Duffy," Robin announced.

Duffy was crossing the Hennesseys' front lawn, wearing a green plastic helmet at a tipsy angle, carrying a plastic sword in one hand and in the other, a large paper sack bulging with the rest of the gear.

"Private Duffy reporting. Ouch!" He had tried to salute with the hand that held the sword and had hit his head with a resounding whap.

"Private Duffy, these are the recruits," said Claudia. "It's our army. Army, this is Private Duffy, except he isn't Private Duffy anymore because I've just promoted him to Colonel Duffy." Duffy beamed.

"What's everybody else?" asked Robby.

"I'm the general," Claudia told him, "and everybody else is a first class private except Leonie, and she's a sergeant."

"That's private first class," Duffy remarked.

"I'd rather be what Claudia says," Robby said, showing Duffy his tongue.

"Well, that's what you are!" Claudia gave Duffy a

stern look. "Okay, now we'll go up to the forest for the drill. Colonel Duffy will hand out the equipment when we get there because this is a secret army." Claudia looked ominously at the circle of faces. "Hey, I almost forgot. Duffy, did you bring the you-know-what?"

Duffy looked blank.

"You know," Claudia insisted, "the pledge."

Duffy replied by fishing out of the sack a newspaper-wrapped article.

"Good," Claudia told him. "Now, army, what Duffy brought is something we all have to bring, something that is very important to us . . . something we like a whole lot."

"Like our ropes?" asked Maurice.

"No, more important than that," Claudia said. "Look, I'm going home to get my important thing. You go and get your important things, too, but remember . . . don't show them to anyone like your mother. Maybe you'd better wrap up what you bring to hide it. I'll get my secret important thing now and go on up to the forest. You all meet here again and come up with Duffy."

"Why can't we all go together?" Leonie asked.

"Because," said Claudia, glancing at Duffy. "Besides, someone has to go ahead and scout, don't they?" Everyone nodded.

Claudia turned and raced toward her house as the rest of them, except for Duffy, ran breathlessly to their respective homes. Holding tight to his sword and paper sack, Duffy sat down with a patient sigh to await their return.

Claudia managed to escape both her mother and Barbara as she ran up to her room. There was no question in her mind as to what she would present as her pledge to secrecy. Not that she really needed one, but it was the fair thing to do.

She went to her small Chinese chest, unlocked it with the key which she kept under the chest, opened it and pulled out a silver chain on which hung a polished piece of gray agate. David had made it for her as a boy scout project and she considered it, next to David's old furniture, the most wonderful thing she had ever owned. She put it in the pocket of her shorts and ran back out, past the Friedmans' lawn where she waved to Duffy, and on up to the forest.

The forest was not really a forest, but a couple of empty lots which had never been cleared of trees and whose owner seemed to have no objection to children playing there.

One particular tree fascinated Claudia because its large roots stuck up out of the ground, making root pockets with the earth. There were several wild, tangled bushes that hovered over it besides, and it made a fine secret hiding place, a good place for the first official meeting of the army. Claudia stood by the tree, waiting for the rest of the army. Soon they appeared, Duffy still lugging his paper sack and the rest of them clutching small newspaper-wrapped parcels. Maurice, Robin, and Robby were giggling.

"All right," Claudia said, "this is going to be our meeting place, here under the bushes."

"Are we going to drill under there?" Leonie asked.

"Leonie, you can't drill under a bush," Claudia explained. "This is just where Duffy will pass out the gear. Follow me." They all went in after her and sat down in a circle. After Claudia had helped herself to the best looking sword and a plastic outer space helmet, Duffy passed out the rest of the plastic swords, rubber daggers, and helmets. It didn't seem to bother Maurice that he ended up with a football helmet, or Robby that they ran out of helmets and he had to wear a baseball catcher's mask instead.

"Now I guess we can have the burial," Claudia said. "Did anyone remember to bring the body?"

Maurice looked as if he were about to cry again. "I forgot," he said.

"I brought it," said Leonie. She held up a folded leaf which she carefully opened up to reveal the squashed caterpillar.

Claudia reviewed it critically. "Okay, Maurice, you can dig the hole."

Maurice began to dig, scratching furiously at the dry dirt with his fingers.

"What are we going to bury him in?" Duffy asked.

"Didn't anyone bring a box?" Claudia stared at

everyone. It seemed that nobody had thought about a box.

"All right," Claudia said briskly, "then we'll have to bury him in a Kleenex." She reached into the pocket of her shorts and pulled out a used paper handkerchief.

"Gee, Claudia," Duffy said, "you can't bury a military hero in a Kleenex."

"What's wrong with it?" Claudia asked him fiercely.

"I don't know, I've just never heard of it before, that's all."

"You're hearing about it now," Claudia told him. "Here, Leonie, wrap him up." She handed Leonie the Kleenex and Leonie carefully folded it around the caterpillar and the leaf. She gave this to Maurice who set it down in the small hole he had dug, shoving some dirt over it.

"Now everybody stand up," Claudia ordered. "At attention!" As they all stood there, stiff and uncomfortable, with their faces scratched by the bushes around them, she sang taps in a clear, flutey voice.

"That was beautiful, Claudia," Leonie whispered.

Claudia drew a circle in the dust with her toe in embarrassment. "Okay, now we have to get on with the business."

"Are you going to tell us the secret?" Leonie asked.

"That's what the business *is*. First, though, we have to give our pledges that we will all keep the army a secret. We'll sit in a circle and take turns showing what we've brought." They all dropped down with a thud. "Duffy, you first."

Duffy carefully opened his package and held up the contents.

"What's *that?*" Claudia asked.

"An electric toothbrush handle," replied Duffy.

"What kind of a secret pledge is *that* . . . an electric toothbrush handle? Holy tomato, Duffy! Is *that* the most important thing you own?"

"Right now it is," Duffy said. "I just got seven cavities filled. The dentist says I may be the first kid in my neighborhood to wear false teeth."

"What if your mom finds out you're not using it?"

"I'll fake it," said Duffy.

"All right," Claudia went on, "who's next. Leonie?"

Leonie shyly opened her package and held up a strand of pearls.

Claudia drew in her breath. "Those aren't real, are they?"

Leonie nodded. "I was going to wear them tomorrow for the first day of school. But I guess I don't have to. Here." She handed them to Claudia.

"Maurice, you're next," Claudia said.

Maurice produced a kind of brass case several inches long and from it drew a paper rolled from both ends toward the middle. He unrolled the paper and held it up before his face so everyone could see it. Everyone could see it, all right, but no one could read it. Half the army, including Maurice, couldn't read anyway, but this looked impossible even to Claudia.

"It's Hebrew," Leonie explained.

"It's my Torah," Maurice added proudly. "I got it because I start first grade tomorrow."

"Is it all right for him to bring that?" Claudia asked Leonie.

"I'm not sure," Leonie replied, "but he said he wouldn't join the army if he couldn't bring it."

"Okay, roll it up and give it to me," Claudia told Maurice. "Robin, you next."

Robin produced her Sunday school attendance card, heavily studded with gold stars. "It shows I went every Sunday last year," she announced. "There's a place for next year, too, and if I get that all filled, I get *two* prizes next summer."

Claudia began to wonder if she, as the leader, should have brought something religious, too, like her little cross on a chain or her Book of Common Prayer. She stopped worrying about this, however, when Robby presented his offering, which was a dead cicada.

"And there's my pledge," she said, displaying her polished agate and feeling pleased that she had brought it when everyone looked impressed.

"What are you going to do with the pledges?" Leonie asked.

"I'm going to do this. I'm going to put everything in this paper sack of Duffy's and then I'm going to hide it under this root by the tree. Next week we'll meet here again and if everyone has kept the secret, I'll give back the pledges and after that we'll just go on our honor."

"But what is the secret?" asked Leonie.

"It's this . . . now put your heads close together . . . what our army is going to do is . . . *spy!*" Claudia ground out the last word, letting her eyes dart around the circle. Maurice gasped.

"Tell them what we're going to spy on," Duffy said.

"We're going to spy on these two girls."

"Why?" asked Robin.

"Just because we are," Claudia said, a reply which seemed quite satisfactory to everyone.

"What two girls, Claudia?" It was Leonie asking.

"Janice Irby and Polly McKisson," replied Claudia. Maurice gasped again.

"Do you know them?" Claudia asked him.

Maurice shook his head.

"I do," said Leonie. "I remember you used to play with Janice. I'll show Maurice who they are when we see them. Robin and Robby, too. Anyway, what are we supposed to do when we spy on them?"

"Just report to me," Claudia told her. "Just report to me every time you see them and tell me what they're doing. And remember, this is a secret. Besides our pledges to keep the secret, we're going to swear on the dead caterpillar that we won't tell about the army. Now, I'm going to put my hand over the caterpillar and everyone put their hands over mine and say after me, 'I swear on this dead hero never to tell.' "

66

"I swear on this dead hero never to tell," they all droned.

"I need to go to the bathroom," said Robby.

"I guess we'd better go home too," Leonie told Claudia. "Momma will be looking for us."

"Okay, we won't drill today."

"When are we going to meet again, Claudia?" Duffy asked. "Tomorrow?"

"No, not tomorrow," Claudia said. "Tomorrow's the first day of school. We'll meet again Saturday morning. I'll let you all know the time. Now remember . . ." she looked pointedly at Maurice, Robin, and Robby, "no squealing. If anyone does, he might not get his pledge back."

"Are we going back together?" Duffy asked.

"No. You all go on ahead. I have to stay here awhile and make plans."

Duffy stayed behind a moment to whisper to Claudia. "What are you going to say if your mother asks if we've been playing together?"

"Look, Duffy, we were not playing together. We were not *playing* together. See?"

"Oh," replied Duffy.

Six

CLAUDIA woke the next morning feeling a warm, heavy lump against her leg. She considered the possibility that her leg might have somehow become broken in her sleep and she could now spend days, maybe even weeks, just lying around the house not going to school. With her eyes still hopefully shut, she moved her leg to see if it hurt. The lump rose up the side of her body, drifted over her shoulder and ended up next to her ear, brushing her hair with its tongue and purring loudly. It was Irma.

For some reason the cat reminded her of a dream she had had that night. In the dream she was throwing balls at two faces painted on a kind of fence; they were the faces of two girls. Each time she hit the fence, two huge, red, blimp-sized tongues would stick out from the faces and make raspberries at her. The raspberries grew very loud and seemed, at last, to wake her up. It was late at night and there were noises at the front door downstairs. She knew then that what had awakened her was not the dream but the noises in the house. She was too sleepy to care about it, though, and was only glad that she had awakened from the bad dream, so she rolled over and went back to sleep. The next thing she knew, there was that lump, Irma.

But now Claudia became curious about the noises. The house sounded terribly ordinary at the moment, her father opening the front door to get the newspaper, her mother preparing breakfast, and Barbara primping in the bathroom, getting ready for school.

School!

Claudia jumped out of bed, scratched her nose as she eyed the rumpled bed, shuffled the blankets around a little and then threw the spread over everything, including Irma, who was curled up by her pillow. The matter of what to wear had all been decided the night before, but Claudia was totally disinterested in the subject because it did not involve shorts or jeans. She dressed hurriedly, ran out the door, stopped, and came back into her room.

Going over to her small Chinese chest, she pulled out from under it a folded piece of paper. This she unfolded and read grimly. At the top of the paper was drawn a skull and crossbones. Beneath it were drawn two large bottles, each with a label across the front. The first label read "Janice Irby's Urp Pills — They Will Make You Urp — Ha!," and the second, "Polly M.'s Pain Pills — They Will *Give* You a Pain — Ha! Ha!" Across the bottom of the paper, Claudia had written "IF YOU TAKE THESE, YOU WILL PROBABLY DIE." Around the edges of the paper, the word "POISON" appeared about twenty times.

Claudia carefully folded the paper back up again, unlocked the chest, and stuffed the paper wad way down into the bottom. Then she locked the chest and continued on her way downstairs.

"This is an unusually early arrival considering it's the first day of school, isn't it?" inquired her father.

Claudia flopped into her chair. "I just wanted to know what those noises were," she said. "I heard noises last night." She glanced suspiciously at both her father and her mother and was disappointed to note that neither one seemed to be hiding anything. Her father, in fact, was yawning.

"I suppose you did. Your brother arrived at the ungodly hour of one thirty."

"David?" Claudia shrieked. "Why didn't anyone tell me? Where is he?"

"We didn't tell you because you just got here," Mrs. Harper said, "and there was not much reason to wake you up in the middle of the night to see a brother who is going to be here a week before he leaves for college."

"And as for where he is right now," Claudia's father

added, "I expect he's pounding the pillow. I would be if I'd been driving for nine hours."

Claudia chewed disconsolately on her cornflakes. "Will he be home when I get home from school?"

"I don't know, dear," Mrs. Harper said. "He's supposed to go fishing with Paul Ingram today, he says, and I don't know when he'll be back."

Claudia groaned. "Fishing?" Not that David would have taken her fishing, anyway, but the thought of David fishing and herself imprisoned at school was terrible. She pondered the injustice of this all the way to school.

Such as it was, though, she would at least have something to do during the day now that she couldn't play with Duffy. Duffy went by bus to a private boys' school two miles away, so there was not much chance of their running into each other, even accidentally. It was funny to think of Duffy being only in the fourth grade. He had enough brains to be in the seventh at least. Claudia wondered how she herself had ever managed to make it to the sixth. Probably, she told herself, because she was a good reader. It certainly wasn't because of *arithmetic*.

Claudia went right to her room when she arrived at school. Nearly all the seats were already filled, but they were filled mostly with strangers who had either been in other rooms the year before or were new to the school. Claudia looked up and down the rows and found only four familiar faces.

One belonged to last year's class clown, a big blond

boy named Bobby Paine. Another face was thin and sallow and seemed to be anchored to its head by a pair of thick, metal-framed glasses. The head, oddly enough, was enormous and was attached to the small, thin body of a boy whose unfortunate last name was Bitty. Claudia could never remember his first name because he had always been called Itty. Itty Bitty was a pet target for Bobby Paine's jokes.

A third person Claudia knew was Jack Sherwood. Claudia would have known who it was even if she couldn't see his face because he always wore blue oxford shirts and a maroon pullover sweater. He was the only one the year before who had passed all the physical fitness tests. The fact that he was also smart didn't impress Claudia nearly so much.

Only one girl was left over from last year, Sarah — Sarah What's-her-name. Sarah was about Claudia's size but had crisp, dark, curly hair and bright pink cheeks which always made her look as if she had just come in from playing in the snow. And she was terrible in sports. In fact, she was nearly always the last one chosen for everything. She and Claudia had hardly exchanged two words all last year. Claudia remembered, though, that Sarah was good in art and always had her pictures on the "best work" board. She was eternally scribbling away in some notebook and didn't seem to care whether she was chosen last or anything. That, Claudia thought, was weird.

After considering her classmates, Claudia turned her attention to their teacher, Mrs. Aiken. It was known around school that Mrs. Aiken had an ulcer, the result probably of worrying about things that didn't worry most teachers — whether the desk a student sat in was the right size for him, for instance. It worried her the first day of school. She was probably worrying about it at that moment, Claudia decided, even before the second bell rang. The desk that Claudia herself sat in was so big that her feet barely touched the floor, so she knew she would get moved.

Just before the second bell rang, when it began to look as if no one else was going to arrive, two girls came in smiling coyly at Mrs. Aiken. They were Janice Irby and Polly McKisson. Claudia nearly fell out of her oversized desk. Why, when there were three other sixth grade classes, did they have to get put in this one — together!

Mrs. Aiken motioned to two empty seats by the window and the girls sidled over and slid in, Polly reviewing the class with her pale blue eyes and registering no expression at all.

The bell rang and the first thing Mrs. Aiken did was ask who felt uncomfortable in his desk and would like to be moved. Half the class raised its hands. There was little left of the next thirty minutes by the time each person thought he felt comfortable. Bobby Paine, warming up to the new class, felt uncomfortable at three different desks. Mrs. Aiken's face was already mapped out with worry lines as she reviewed the class. Claudia tried to look indifferent and comfortable in her oversized desk. She was exactly across the room from Janice and Polly and she intended to stay there.

"Now, is everyone comfortable?" Mrs. Aiken asked.

Claudia nodded along with the rest of the class. She even tried smiling comfortably, which only had the unfortunate effect of drawing Mrs. Aiken's attention to her.

"Now, what is *your* name?" Mrs. Aiken asked.

"Claudia Harper," said Claudia, trying to look as large as possible.

"Claudia, I don't believe that desk does fit you."

"It fits me fine, Mrs. Aiken," Claudia said quickly, too quickly.

"Well," Mrs. Aiken said with a friendly smile, "I don't believe it really does. Let me see now." She studied the room. "There, that one looks right." She pointed to the only empty desk in the room which was directly behind Janice, and Janice was directly across from Polly.

Claudia groaned audibly. "I'd rather not sit by the window. It . . . it hurts my eyes. Couldn't we move the desk here?"

"Well now, if the light continues to hurt your eyes, we'll do something about it. In the meantime, it's easier to move Muhammad to the mountain than the mountain to Muhammad, isn't it?"

Claudia could hardly argue with that, so she stood up and marched across the room to her new desk. On her way she saw Janice and Polly raising their eyebrows at each other, Polly sticking out her tongue, and Janice daintily putting her fingers on her nose. It was a warm welcome.

For nearly an hour, Claudia developed a stiff neck trying to keep her eyes away from the back of Janice's head. Then, at last, the thought occurred to her that this was much worse for Janice and Polly than it was for her. After all, she had formed a whole army for the sole purpose of spying on them, and here she had been placed in a perfect spying position with no effort at all. Having developed this idea, Claudia began to enjoy herself. It was really quite fascinating watching Janice and Polly flapping their eyebrows at each other over everything that happened in class. It was too bad they didn't give a grade in eyebrows or they would surely have had an A. Tee, hee, hee — an A in eyebrows!

And there was no doubt that Claudia's being there made both girls uncomfortable. Yes, indeed, Claudia was going to enjoy this.

About midmorning, Mrs. Aiken asked who "brought" or who "bought" lunch. This question was asked every day for the school cafeteria. Each one in the class would raise his hand and then look around to see what everyone else was doing. It was almost like choosing up for teams. Claudia always "brought" except on days when a previous week's school bulletin had announced that they were having grilled cheese sandwiches or hamburgers or spaghetti on the menu.

Janice and Polly both raised their hands, and their eyebrows, of course, for "bought." At lunchtime Claudia saw them slide chummily through the cafeteria line as she found a place at a table where everyone was unpacking either a brown paper sack or a lunch box. She was sitting right next to Sarah What's-her-name.

Claudia pulled her peanut-butter sandwich out of her lunch box and noticed that Sarah was having a peanut-butter sandwich too. Claudia loved peanut butter and, as her family said, did everything but take a bath in it. Mrs. Harper always bought the old-fashioned kind that had the oil floating on top. This was supposed to be better for you. At one time she had become terribly excited over some book on nutrition and began feeding the family all kinds of strange food. As Claudia remembered it, they nearly died from nutrition. The only thing still remaining from this nutrition experiment was the peanut butter, although it was pretty good even if it was like chewing glue.

She watched as Sarah wrinkled up her nose at her own sandwich. "What's wrong?" she asked.

Sarah threw a quick look around the table. "Wheat germ in my peanut butter," she hissed under her breath. Claudia hardly blamed her for wanting to keep this information private. It was not the kind of thing a person would broadcast at a school lunch table.

"Ugh!" Claudia offered sympathetically. "I had that stuff for about two months last year. Also things like yoghurt and black strap molasses. It was sickening!"

"I agree," said Sarah. "I wonder if it will ever end. I mean, how did it end at *your* house?"

"We kind of went on strike. My father said he couldn't see any difference between dying of malnutrition or dying of starvation. You were just as dead either way, but it was more fun to die of malnutrition. Then I guess my mother gave the book away."

"I might just try that," said Sarah.

"What, dying of malnutrition or starvation?"

"No, giving the book away." Sarah started to giggle.

"What's funny?" Claudia asked.

"That thing you said about dying of malnutrition or starvation. That's what's funny."

Claudia grinned. "I guess it is," she said.

And it was funny too, she told herself, that here they were, having this conversation over wheat germ and peanut butter (of all things!) as if they had been friends for years, the kind of conversation she often had with Duffy. And they had hardly spoken together before in their whole lives. It really was amazing.

After lunch they walked out to the playground together. Several games were already in progress and somebody, two people in fact, called out to Claudia to join their game of dodgeball.

When Claudia was back at her desk after the lunch period, she couldn't think why she had been so rude. She had really wanted to do something with Sarah, to talk with her some more, but when they had called to her, all she could think of was joining the game and she had dashed off without a word to Sarah. She remembered that Sarah had simply stood and stared after her for a moment and then turned and walked away. No one asked Sarah to join in on a game, but then they rarely did.

Claudia tried telling herself that it wasn't her fault Sarah was so terrible at sports, but it didn't help. What she remembered mostly was that Sarah hadn't smiled at her when she walked into the classroom, but had just picked up her notebook and started drawing in it.

Seven

CLAUDIA raced home after school, anxious to change into "something decent" in the way of shorts, and then sneak around in the hope of meeting Duffy secretly. She had no intention of *playing* with him, of course. They were just going to discuss army business.

She plunged through the front door, nearly falling over Irma, who was waiting for someone to let her out. "Come on, Irma!" she said, gently helping Irma out the door with the toe of her shoe.

"Greetings!" came a voice from the couch.

"David!" Claudia shrieked. Then, "I thought you were going fishing." It was a lame thing to say when you hadn't seen someone in two months, but it was all Claudia could think of at the moment.

"I was. Too tired." David yawned and threw the book he was reading down on the floor. "How's by you, pest?"

"Fine," said Claudia. "Hey, are you going fishing tomorrow?" Another lame thing to say.

"Maybe. And then again . . . say, would it ruin your life if I said I might never go fishing again?" A sudden, teasing grin crossed David's face. It was a grin Claudia loved. "My, young lady," David went on, "how you have grown. Why, I do believe you have added a whole millionth of an inch to the top of your haid. That is head, ma'am."

Claudia curtseyed. "Thank you kindly. And would you allow that I am getting to be a very big girl?"

"I would also allow that, ma'am," said David, eyeing Claudia appraisingly.

"That's very nicely of you, Brother David," Claudia said. She started to pirouette in front of him, whirling around until she grew dizzy and fell in a heap on the floor, giggling into the rug.

David suddenly became serious and leaned over toward her. "Hey, I don't want to bring up anything unpleasant, but are you in some kind of trouble, pest?"

Claudia had to stop and think this over a moment because she was never quite sure whether she was in trouble or not. "I don't think so."

"Well, Mom's waiting for you to come home, if you know what I mean. She's been getting some telephone calls today and I think they were about you. Anyway, brace yourself." David picked his book up off the floor.

"Okay." Claudia jumped up. "Here goes!" she said, running out.

At the kitchen door she stood watching her mother peel potatoes. For some reason, her mother was not using the peeler, but was carving off the peel with a knife. Claudia stood hypnotized by the thin, neat corkscrews of peel falling from the potato. At last her mother noticed her.

"Hello, dear, how was your first day of school?" She smiled a little absently, certainly not looking mad about anything. Claudia decided that David must have been in a big flap about nothing.

"Fine," she said, pulling a bottle of milk from the refrigerator and pouring herself a glass.

Mrs. Harper continued to peel. "By the way, I received some strange phone calls today. You wouldn't by any chance know the whereabouts of an electric toothbrush handle, a string of pearls, and a Sunday school attendance record, would you?"

"Who wants to know?" Claudia asked, wiping a milk mustache off on her arm.

"Well, Mrs. Booth is looking for Duffy's electric toothbrush handle. Mrs. Friedman is looking for Leonie's string of pearls, *real* pearls, and Mrs. Hennessey, for Robin's Sunday school attendance record."

Claudia had another gulp of milk. "Why did they call here?"

"Mrs. Booth just called here on general principles. I haven't said anything to her about the fact that we think you and Duffy shouldn't be playing so much together."

"So much?" squealed Claudia.

Mrs. Harper continued calmly, quite unmoved. "I should have said 'at all.' Mrs. Friedman and Mrs. Hennessey both mentioned that they thought you were playing with the children yesterday."

"The kids didn't say anything?" Claudia asked.

"Not that I know of," replied her mother, peeling steadily away.

"Not even Robby and Maurice?"

Mrs. Harper put down her knife and whirled around to face Claudia. "What exactly do you mean . . . not even Robby and Maurice?"

"Nothing. I didn't mean anything."

"All right, young lady," said Mrs. Harper, "I want to know exactly what you know about all this. I thought I saw your hand in it, but I was trying to give you the benefit of the doubt. However, when I get three telephone calls about, of all things, an electric toothbrush handle, a string of pearls, a Sunday school record, and a . . . a . . ."

"Torah!" Claudia burst in helpfully, then immediately put her hand to her mouth.

"I suspected you'd know about that, too. Claudia, I'm not going to ask the reason behind all this. All I'm going to ask is that you march to . . . to wherever all this strange assortment of articles is being stored, bring them to me to be checked, and then take them back where they belong. Are they up in your room?"

Claudia stared at the floor. "No."

"Well, I don't need to pry into where they are. Just please go and get them and bring them here."

"Now?"

"Of course, *now*."

Claudia set down her empty glass and headed for the door.

"Claudia?"

Claudia stopped at the door and waited for her mother to speak.

"There's just one more thing. You didn't *take* these things, did you?"

Claudia lowered her head, her face turning scarlet. "No."

"I'll accept your word for that," said Mrs. Harper. "Now hurry, please."

Claudia ran, but even running, it seemed to take forever to get to the forest. Still, she was able to keep from crying. There were still children coming home from school, and she would rather have been caught dead than crying.

The brown paper sack was there where they had left it. It looked like a strange fungus growing from the root of the tree. Claudia was almost afraid to touch it, but she picked it up gingerly and ran home, not even looking to see if all the things were still in it. She had done nothing dishonest, but suddenly she *felt* dishonest, an escaped criminal pointed at by the windows of the houses she passed.

Barbara and David were in the kitchen with Mrs. Harper when Claudia returned. Barbara was reading the comics on the table and David was leaning back against the wall, lighting up a pipe. This was something new, David smoking a pipe. Claudia stared at him as she stood in the doorway with the paper sack clutched in her arm.

"Welcome," David said. Barbara simply looked up at her and then went back to the paper.

"Well?" said Mrs. Harper.

"Well, what?" replied Claudia.

"Well, let's see what you have in the sack."

"Here?" asked Claudia.

"Why not here?"

"Couldn't we go up to my room?" Claudia asked.

"I'm just too busy getting dinner, Claudia. Now just empty the sack on the kitchen table, please."

Claudia's lips tightened as she went to the table, but she said nothing. Her mother, David, and Barbara all watched her as she slowly took each thing out of the sack and set it down.

Everything was there, the electric toothbrush handle, the string of pearls, the Torah, the Sunday school attendance record, the dead cicada, and Claudia's own polished agate on a chain. Each had seemed so serious, so important, when it had been part of the ceremony. Now, with strange eyes staring, the things looked naked and sad and lonely. They looked comic.

Barbara snickered.

"Shut up, Barb," David said.

"Well, what *is* all that?" Barbara returned.

Their mother's face suddenly looked strained, as if she might have made a mistake about something. "That is not your concern, Barbara. It's just . . . it's just something Claudia has to attend to. I think Claudia knows what she has to do."

"Hmmmph!" Barbara snorted.

"Isn't that the agate I made for you?" David asked.

Claudia nodded, picking it up and hanging it around her neck. Then she took up the other things, stuffed them back in the sack, and turned to go.

"Look, pest," David offered, "do you want me to go with you to do whatever it is you have to do?"

"I guess not, thanks," Claudia said, her eyes turned from him. No one else said anything as she left.

When she returned about ten minutes later with the empty, crushed sack, David intercepted her as she passed the living room door.

"Hey, sport," he called out, "wait a minute!"

Claudia stood looking at him for a moment, then she entered the living room.

"Look, pest, what's with you and Duffy?" David asked.

"What's what with me and Duffy?"

"Mom says you're not supposed to be playing with him. Were you playing with him?"

Claudia stared at the coffee table and said nothing.

"Mom's not stupid, you know," David continued.

"Okay, let's put it this way. Do you know why you're not supposed to be playing with him?"

"Because I'm an eleven-year-old girl and he's an eight-year-old boy and when we play together, we play together too much and we get into mischief and stuff and I get into trouble." Claudia recited all this as if it were a poem she had memorized.

"Okay, okay . . . you got the picture. Look, peanut, you know everyone likes Duffy."

"I know," Claudia said.

"It's just that they think you should be playing more with girls your own age. Look, isn't there anyone . . . I mean how about that Janice you used to run around with. Mom says she's back."

"She is but she's . . . she's busy," Claudia said.

"How busy?"

"Busy," said Claudia.

"Oh." David continued puffing on his pipe. Then he said suddenly, as if he had just drawn an inspiration from the little bursts of smoke, "Well, isn't there anyone else in school?"

"Sure. There're lots of people in school."

"Okay, maybe you'll meet someone new this year that you like."

"Maybe," Claudia said. "But they probably won't live around here."

David shrugged. "So import them!"

Claudia examined the pattern on the rug, following the spiral lines around and around. Like the conversation, they weren't really going anyplace.

Finally she broke her own silence. "Things always have to change. Everything always has to change."

"*Every*thing doesn't change, sport," David said. "And it would be pretty boring if some things didn't, wouldn't it?"

"But why is it when things change, it's always to get worse?"

"Heck, Claudia, that's a pretty crazy thing to think. Maybe it's just that those are the only changes you're noticing right now."

"Maybe," Claudia said. "But why do *people* have to change?"

"Some people don't. Kids grow up, though, and that's changing. Is growing up what you're talking about?"

"I guess so."

"I don't think growing up is a bad change. You wouldn't want to stay a kid all your life, would you?"

"I guess not. But why does everyone have to grow up exactly the same way?"

"I wasn't aware that everyone had to."

"That's because you're a boy and you can grow up the way you want to. You can even smoke a pipe and no one says anything!"

"Were you planning to take up pipe-smoking?" David asked.

Claudia gave an impatient sigh. "What I'm *trying* to say is why can't I play with Duffy? Why can't I grow up the way I want to? Why . . . why . . .

why do I have to *walk up the stairs the way Janice does!*"

David's eyes opened at this. Then he grinned. "Well, I don't know about Janice, but as for Duffy, that's Mom and Dad's idea. If you want to know my private opinion, I don't see why you can't play with him, either."

He continued to grin at Claudia until she was forced to grin back.

"David! David!" she cried, running up to him. "David, please can we play checkers together tonight after dinner?"

"Heck, pest, I can't. I'm taking Claire out to dinner tonight. Hey, could we make it another night?"

Before Claudia went to sleep that night, she lay on her stomach for a long time, hands under chin, staring at the bedstead. She wondered if perhaps she should have given her prayer book as a pledge instead of the agate. Perhaps God was mad at her. Perhaps he would arrange for David to be busy every night until he left for college. But then if she *had* left the prayer book, it wasn't the most important thing she had, so wouldn't that have been like lying? Did God want her to lie? Anyway, she had not been *playing* with Duffy, she told herself right out of the blue. And then suddenly, without quite knowing why, she found that she was crying.

Eight

EVERYONE was in the kitchen but David when Claudia came down for breakfast the next morning. Mr. Harper was leaning on the counter reading the paper and drinking his first cup of coffee. He always poured the first cup himself and then couldn't wait to sit down before he drank it. Mrs. Harper was scrambling eggs and Barbara was sitting at the table, yawning. It seemed unbelievable, Claudia thought, that her secret army had almost been blasted off the face of the earth and everyone was going on as if nothing had ever happened. The whole world was probably going on as if nothing had happened. A whole world full of fathers guzzling their morning coffee, a whole world full of mothers scrambling eggs, and a whole world full of ugly sisters sitting and yawning at a whole world full of breakfast tables. Claudia sat down with a plunk, knocking the table as she did so.

"If you *don't* mind!" Barbara said, glaring at her.

"*What* is the matter?" asked Mrs. Harper.

"Oh, it's just Claudia," Barbara grumbled. "She's about as graceful as an eleven-year-old baby elephant."

Mr. Harper winked at Claudia. "I've heard that this is a good year for eleven-year-old baby elephants." Claudia giggled.

"Speaking of baby elephants," said Mrs. Harper, "what I mean is . . . oh dear, I don't know what I mean. Anyway, Mrs. Irby telephoned me yesterday, Claudia."

Claudia was dying to know what Mrs. Irby wanted but she wasn't going to say so.

"Don't you want to know why she called?" asked her mother.

"I guess so," Claudia said as she stirred diligently around in the jam jar to find a whole strawberry.

"Somebody make her stop! She's poisoning the strawberry jam," moaned Barbara.

"Claudia, stop poisoning the strawberry jam," said Mr. Harper. This made Claudia giggle again.

"What Mrs. Irby called to say, *Claudia*," Mrs. Harper interrupted firmly, "was that Janice is planning a little party and you'll probably be invited to it. Isn't that nice?"

"Me!" shrieked Claudia.

"Why not you?"

"She's lying!"

"Claudia!"

"Well, she is! Janice wouldn't invite me to a . . . a dog fight!"

"Oh, she might do that. She might ask you to a dog fight," Barbara said. "Even *I* might do that!"

"You just . . . you just shut up!" Claudia bellowed at her.

"All right, Claudia," said Mr. Harper. "I don't want to hear that expression again. You know it gives your mother a pain in the ear. Once more and you may excuse yourself from the table."

"What's the matter, dear?" Mrs. Harper asked. "What happened between you and Janice?"

"Nothing," Claudia said.

"I'll bet something happened," Barbara said.

"Well, I'm not going! There won't be anyone there but a bunch of horsey petunias and I'm not going!"

"What kind of an expression is that?" asked Mrs. Harper with a look of horror.

"Sounds like twentieth-century Duffy to me," said Mr. Harper drily.

"I think it sounds . . . dirty," Barbara offered.

"Well, I don't like the sound of it, wherever it came from, and until we look into it further, I don't want to hear it again! Besides, this whole discussion is academic, which means, Claudia, that whether you like it or not, if you receive an invitation to Janice's party, you are going."

Claudia groaned. "If you want to know what I think . . ."

"We don't," said Barbara.

"If you want to know what I think," Claudia began again, "I think this whole party is Mrs. Irby's idea. I think *Mrs. Irby* is the one who's inviting me. I think . . ."

"As a matter of fact, dear, it might have been Mrs. Irby's idea, whatever difference that makes. It's nice of her to want you."

"Who knows, they might even have boys," Barbara said. "Janice is already twelve, isn't she?"

"Boys?" Claudia said brightly.

"I mean, for *dancing*," Barbara said.

"Dancing!" shrieked Claudia.

"Keep your voice down, dear," said Mrs. Harper. "No, Barbara, I don't believe there will be boys, for dancing or anything else. Mrs. Irby apparently suggested this party so that Janice could get reacquainted with all the little girl friends she used to have."

"Ha!" said Claudia.

All the way to school that day, she tried to think of a good reason for not going to the party. At last she settled on kidney trouble. This was something a friend of her mother's was always complaining about and it sounded like a good kind of illness to suddenly develop. How would anybody know if you *didn't* have it? Claudia felt considerably better after reaching this decision.

She very nearly forgot about the party, however, because Janice, of course, said nothing about it. And school went on as usual.

Mrs. Aiken announced that the girls would have Miss Murdock again for physical education. This was supposed to be cheerful news because there had been some question about Miss Murdock's returning that year. Claudia did not feel very cheerful about it.

Also that morning they found out that they were going to have a man, Mr. Dalroy, for art. Claudia remembered seeing a man wandering about the halls that morning looking a little lost. She decided that that must have been Mr. Dalroy when she heard a sigh from several girls around her, namely Janice Irby and Polly McKisson. The man Claudia had seen had been tall, with tremendous, football-sized shoulders. Also he was blond and wore a tweed jacket.

Bobby Paine developed a coughing fit when Mrs. Aiken made the announcement. So did the rest of the boys, including Itty Bitty, who unfortunately began to choke. Mrs. Aiken excused him to go to the water fountain for a drink. By the time he returned, the excitement over Mr. Dalroy had ended, but Bobby Paine put out his foot and tripped Itty as he went back to his desk across the aisle. Then he leaned over and poked him with a pencil. Then he blew a few spitballs at him.

The last spitball hit Itty on the ear and he yelled "Ouch!"

"Shut up!" Bobby hissed at him, but it was too late. Bobby had already distinguished himself with Mrs. Aiken by having his desk changed so many times, and other things, so she lost no time in ordering him to bring his books up to the reading table at the front of the room.

"Just you wait!" Bobby whispered to Itty on his way up. Itty looked so scared that Claudia thought his large head would fall right off his thin neck and roll on the floor. She wished that Itty would get brave and sock Bobby on the arm as he walked by, but Itty didn't. Once Bobby got himself settled, with much shifting of books, his chair, and himself, the class forgot about the whole thing.

Mr. Dalroy arrived for art just before the lunch period. They had never had a man for art before, or for any other class for that matter, and Claudia was fascinated. It was especially fascinating to watch the mooney looks Janice and Polly gave each other. She couldn't see Janice's face, but the back of her neck certainly looked mooney. Actually, it was more sickening than fascinating.

Claudia knew that Sarah would end up being the best art student in class, but Mr. Dalroy couldn't know it on the first day. He gave a lot of special help to Janice and Polly simply because they kept going up to ask. Also they stayed, simpering, after class to talk to him. It really was sickening.

Claudia had lunch with a girl named Alice Clay. She had considered going over to sit with Sarah, but Sarah had looked at her so blankly as she approached the table that she had veered away and found the empty place next to Alice. Was Sarah really mad at her because she had run off to join that game?

That was one good thing about Duffy. You always knew where you stood with Duffy. If only Duffy were eleven years old and a girl and in sixth grade and in Mrs. Aiken's class. That was a lot of ifs. Anyway, if he were all those things, Claudia decided, she probably wouldn't like him. That was the way life was. She finished her peanut-butter sandwich and went out to the playground with Alice.

They were standing at the foot of the cement stairs when Claudia heard Bobby Paine's voice. "You'd *better* take them off!" The words were low pitched and nasty.

The girls looked back into the shadows where the stairs connected to the school building and saw Bobby standing there with his back to them. Facing him, with his back pressed up tight against the wall, was Itty Bitty. With his glasses shining against his face, he looked like a petrified white owl.

"No," he said in a small, queer voice.

"Look, you take them off or I'll take them off for you!" Bobby moved closer to Itty.

"Maybe we'd better call someone," Alice whispered to Claudia.

Claudia, for just a moment, considered going up and pushing Bobby away, maybe even hitting him. She was sure that talking wouldn't do any good. He sounded too mean. But Claudia was scared. She was angry, too, but more scared than angry. It was probably the way Itty felt, scared and angry, a terrible way to feel. Claudia looked desperately around for someone to ask for help. Bobby was a big sixth-grader and you would need someone at least as big as he was to do any good.

Then Claudia found her eyes drawn to something she would have recognized anywhere, a blue shirt with a maroon sweater slung over the shoulders. She raced over to it.

"Jack, quick! Bobby's going to fight Itty!"

"Where?" Jack Sherwood asked.

"Under the steps! Hurry!" Claudia ran back with Jack right behind her. She waited at the foot of the steps with Alice as Jack went in and yanked Bobby away.

"Look, lay off him!" Jack said.

"You keep out of it!" Bobby snarled back.

"I said *lay off!*" Jack Sherwood was at least as big as Bobby Paine and everyone knew he was the best athlete in school. Bobby sneered at him, put his hands in his pockets and slouched away. Itty continued to stand there, looking as if he actually had been hit, as if he might be going to cry. Jack patted him on the shoulder and turned away.

"Let's go," Claudia said. She didn't want to be around if Itty should start to cry. It would be terrible for Itty.

Claudia thought a lot about Itty, wondering when she went to bed that night if she might have a nightmare about his scared owl face. She had thought she might talk about it to David when she returned from school, but David was out and was still out at her bedtime. She had even sneaked around trying to see Duffy, just to take her mind off it. But Duffy wasn't in the tree and she wouldn't have dared ring the doorbell and ask for him.

What did you do when you wanted to talk to someone and didn't have anyone to talk to? When Claudia was little, she had made up a friend once. She had kept the friend so long that her mother had taken her to see Dr. Bauman about it. Made-up friends didn't work when you were eleven. And if you did make one up, what would your parents do about *that*? Ha! Right into the straitjacket!

Claudia wondered if she would have any time at all with David before he left. He was gone that night. He would probably be gone the next night and the next. On Saturday morning, he would be leaving for college. And some day soon, he would be leaving home forever.

Of course, Claudia still had David's room and his

old furniture. Furniture didn't grow up and leave home. Perhaps it was the only thing in the whole world you could really count on. That was funny, having your best friends in the whole world be pieces of furniture. But if it was so funny, why were her eyes stinging? Was she going to cry after all? It seemed that once you started crying about things, you kept right on crying about them — like David leaving, and Itty, and not being allowed to play with Duffy, and some dumb girl who was terrible in sports anyway not smiling at you, and having a war with someone who used to be your best friend.

Anyway, Claudia told herself that she was simply not going to cry. The thing to do was to count to ten and change the subject.

So Claudia counted to ten. And then twenty. And then all the way to one hundred. But when she finally fell asleep, her pillow was wet, anyway.

Nine

THE NEXT DAY, the girls had physical education period with Miss Murdock. Mrs. Aiken's room met with the girls from another sixth grade room on the blacktop between the playing field and the school building.

Miss Murdock never simply stood around waiting for them. She was always throwing baskets or leaping around doing something. You could see her as you walked out, bouncing around in her white blouse and black skirt like a two-colored kangaroo, the large whistle she wore around her neck swinging madly back and forth. She even bounced athletically up and down on the balls of her feet when she addressed the girls. Her skin was always the color of skimmed milk and her eyes turned watery and pink-rimmed in the wind. Claudia had once thought she might want to be a gym teacher, but that was before she met Miss Murdock.

It was hot out, but they had to do warm-up exercises, anyway. Miss Murdock did warm-up exercises as if the life of the whole school depended on it.

One, two, flap, flap.

Three, four, flop, flop.

Kick, kick, five, six.

Touch your toes, ah, ah, ah.

To the right waist bend, ah, ah.

To the left waist bend, ah, ah.

Further, further, bend, bend, bend.

Somebody bent so far over she fell down completely, but Miss Murdock went right on singing out commands. Holy tomato, Claudia thought, she's hypnotized herself! It was like being in the British Guards where you couldn't lean down to help a fallen comrade in a parade. Holy tomato!

After everyone was warmed up and exhausted, they had a lecture on sportsmanship and fair play. This left only about ten minutes for a game.

"Now," said Miss Murdock with a brisk smile in all directions, "we are going to choose up sides for teams." It sounded as if she expected everyone to cheer. "You and you may be captains." She pointed toward Claudia and Janice who were standing on opposite ends of the front row.

Somebody raised her hand. "Are we going to have

the same captain and teams all term, Miss Murdock?"

Another thirty seconds went by as Miss Murdock considered this question. "No, this will just be for to-day."

Choosing up teams was ridiculous because it left no time to play a game. Claudia raised her hand. "Couldn't we just number off and play odds and evens? It would be faster." A few voices shouted "Yea!"

One voice, however, said, "I think we should choose the way Miss Murdock says." It was Janice Irby.

Miss Murdock fumbled with her whistle for a moment, then she smiled serenely. "I believe we shall still choose up teams."

Janice looked around triumphantly and Claudia glared. She knew that the only reason Janice wanted to choose anything was so that she could choose Polly, never mind whether they played a game or not.

Miss Murdock pointed to Claudia. "You may go first," she said. It was a remarkably clear case of appeasement, but it didn't make Claudia feel any better. Janice had had her way, and there would be little, if any, time left for a game.

Claudia looked up and down the rows of girls. "I choose . . . I choose . . . *Polly McKisson.*" Claudia could hardly believe that she could be so clever as to suddenly think of this.

Janice turned a furious red, and Miss Murdock had to remind her that it was her turn. Claudia simply looked at both Janice and Polly with an innocent, angelic look on her face.

Another problem still remained, however. Claudia wondered if she should choose Sarah and perhaps straighten everything out, if there was anything to be straightened. But when she looked at Sarah, Sarah just looked back at her in that strange, blank way, as if they had never spoken at the lunch table. If Sarah was going to stay mad, then let her, Claudia told herself. She hesitated for a moment and then chose a girl standing next to her whom she didn't even know.

When the bell rang, four girls still hadn't been chosen, but Miss Murdock dismissed the class with an athletic fweep on her whistle anyway. It was amazing. Claudia wondered if the whole year was going to be spent in choosing up teams for the sole purpose of choosing up teams. It really was amazing. Claudia looked back as they returned to the building and saw that Miss Murdock was already hopping around tossing balls into the basket. Her huge whistle flew up and hit her in the eye, but she didn't even seem to feel it.

For the rest of the day, notes flew at an unbelievable rate between the desks of Janice Irby and Polly McKisson. Claudia was so curious she could hardly breathe. At last she was able to intercept one.

Neither Janice nor Polly knew that she had the note. Mrs. Aiken called them to attention at the very moment that Polly had slipped the note across the floor toward Janice. Claudia stealthily put out her foot and slid it back to her own desk.

The note read: "You don't think she'll actually come? How can she come when she doesn't have a u-no-what?" Much to Claudia's surprise, this had nothing to do with the physical education period at all.

But, u-no-what what? What were they talking about? Aha! The party! She was being invited to a party she couldn't come to because she didn't have a u-no-what. Claudia had no doubt at all that the "she" was herself. She didn't have to invent kidney trouble after all. But what was to be accomplished by not going to a party if they didn't want you, anyway? The kidney trouble, at least was her idea. It was all so confusing that Claudia had to think about it awhile.

In the meantime, still consumed with curiosity, she slipped the note into her book bag to take home. She planned to keep this together with her "poison" paper as evidence, evidence of what she didn't know. When the invitation to whatever it was came, she might be able to figure the whole thing out.

A small pink envelope was sitting perched up against her mother's glass sugar canister when Claudia came in from school. She threw her book bag on the kitchen table and ran toward it, but when she saw her mother, who was at the moment washing out Irma's milk dish, watching her, she sauntered over to the cupboard instead and pulled out a glass.

"I think that's for you, dear," said Mrs. Harper. "It's probably Janice's invitation. How was school today?" She leaned over and kissed Claudia on the cheek as Claudia passed her on the way to the refrigerator.

"Oh, fine," Claudia said.

"Well, aren't you going to open it?"

"Oh, sure," Claudia said. She polished the outside of the glass on her shirt, opened the refrigerator door, and took out the milk, pouring it into her glass with deliberate care. Ordinarily she sloshed it all over the place, as her mother well knew. She took a sip of the milk and picked up the envelope, reading the address as if to make sure it was for her. Then she took a knife from the drawer and carefully slit open the top of the envelope, something she had never done in her life before. Her mother looked at her and sighed. Then she nearly dropped Irma's dish as Claudia roared, "Well!"

"Claudia, please!" she said. Then, her face curious, "Well what?"

"Well *well!*" replied Claudia, dropping down into a kitchen chair with a resounding thud. "So that's it!"

"So what's it?" asked Mrs. Harper, thoroughly exasperated. "Are you or are you not going to tell me what it is, Claudia?"

"Do you remember what I said about this party being Mrs. Irby's idea?"

"Yes, I suppose so. And I agreed that it might be."

"Well, the party may be Mrs. Irby's idea, but *this* is Janice's idea!" Claudia looked triumphantly at her mother, as if the whole thing was her mother's fault.

"Dear, will you please tell me what's in the invitation so that we can at least discuss it intelligently. And also, please don't act as if you were challenging me to a duel."

Claudia paid no attention to the last remark, but began to read out loud with elaborate care, "You and your *dog* are invited to a garden party at my house Saturday, September 20, from three to five. You have to bring a dog with you because this is a tea party for pets. I hope you can come. Janice Irby." Claudia banged the invitation down on the table. "Ha!"

"You don't need to get violent," Mrs. Harper reminded her. "Why I think that's a very nice little invitation. Just what do you find wrong with it?"

"What's wrong with it is that they don't want me to come!" Claudia did not intend showing her mother the note from Polly to Janice she had intercepted. Anyway, the invitation for her *not* to come was clear enough.

"Now how did you get an idea like that?" asked Mrs. Harper, to Claudia's complete amazement. "Janice sent you the invitation, didn't she? Why would she send you an invitation if she didn't want you to come?"

"Because Mrs. Irby made her!" shouted Claudia. "But the dog idea is Janice's and Janice knows I don't have a dog. Now just where am I going to get a dog to take to the party? I ask you . . . where is *my* dog?" She stared accusingly at her mother. The fact was that Claudia had been begging for a puppy ever since their Dalmatian had died three years before, and it suddenly seemed like a good time to bring the whole matter up again.

"Well, dear, you can take . . . that is you can take . . . well, I guess you really don't have a dog to take, do you?" Mrs. Harper's voice trailed away.

Claudia waited hopefully for her mother to suggest that they race down to the pet shop and pick up a puppy immediately, but all her mother did was take up the invitation and read it over again to herself. "Well, after all, it does say *pets* here. Perhaps you could take . . . no, what am I thinking of. You couldn't very well take a *cat* to a party where there are going to be dogs."

Claudia caught herself from saying, "Why not?" as that would only have brought on a pointless argument. But she did say, "Well then . . . I'm not going!"

Mrs. Harper looked her straight in the eye. "As I said this morning, you *are* going!" This on a very firm note.

"You mean you're going to get me a puppy?" asked Claudia.

"No, you are going with*out* a dog," replied her mother.

106

"They won't let me in."

"Don't be silly. Of course, they'll let you in. I'm sure it's all just in fun, anyway. But if you like, I'll telephone Mrs. Irby and explain . . ." She stopped because Claudia was shaking her head violently.

The kitchen grew quiet. Claudia listened for a while to the buzzing of the electric clock, thinking, for some reason, of her mother's vague suggestion that she take Irma to the party. One thought led to another and, "Oh, all right," she said. "I'll go."

U-no-what, indeed! she told herself. She would have a u-no-what, all right. She might even have several. Acquiring the u-no-whats, however, involved having conferences with some people she knew, and the sooner the better. She studied her empty glass of milk for a moment and then leaped up from the table, heading for the back door.

"Now where are you off to?" Mrs. Harper asked. "You just got here."

"I guess I'll skate awhile," replied Claudia.

"Without your skates?" asked her mother.

"Oh," said Claudia, changing course and heading for her room. She remembered now to take her book bag because she wanted to remove the note and lock it in the chest as soon as possible.

Once back outside, the note safely locked away and herself comfortably changed into her torn-off jeans and David's old shirt, she put on her skates and skated leisurely down the drive and in a direction away from Duffy's house. Finally, after touring the block about three times, she glanced toward the apple tree in Duffy's yard and saw a leg hanging down from the lowest branch.

With a casual glance toward her own house to make sure no one was looking out the window, Claudia quickly turned into the Booths' driveway and skated up to the fence.

Ten

CLAUDIA surprised everyone by announcing Saturday morning that she was going to take a bath. This was a surprise because she'd had one the night before. Mrs. Harper asked her if she remembered it and Claudia did. Mr. Harper reminded her that her skin might wrinkle up so she would look like a prune, and Barbara said that she already *did* look like a prune. Barbara also told her to remember to clean out the bathtub because she did not wish to have *her* bath surrounded by Claudia's ring of dirt.

Claudia rose up the stairs with her nose in the air, totally offended. She told no one that her reason for doing this startling thing was that she needed a very strong charm, something more than crossing fingers or wearing a rabbit's foot or rubbing her left thumb around the right newel post three times. The charm needed to be something special, something she didn't ordinarily do. The Saturday bath was to insure that her plan for the party worked.

Claudia went to her room and took her terry cloth bathrobe from the closet. Then she collected a nail file and her plastic brush and comb set from the top drawer of her chest of drawers. As she turned to leave, she remembered something else and returned to the closet, from which she emerged with her tin of baby powder. Thus armed, she strode purposefully to the bathroom, the tail of her bathrobe sash trailing on the floor.

Once in the bathroom, she carefully locked herself in, set all her gear on the floor and turned on the water full force. The steam rose up in gusts as she peeled off her clothes. Watching it, she had another idea. Opening the cabinet over the basin, she pulled down a large lavender box belonging to Barbara and read the directions. They informed her that she was to use one tablespoon per tub, but not knowing quite how much one tablespoon was, Claudia tilted the box over the bath water and poured about one cup's worth. She watched dreamily as the tub filled with bubbles.

Before climbing into the tub, Claudia had still another idea. Barbara's frilly white shower cap hung on the shower head. Claudia had never considered anything so dumb as a shower cap in her life, but today she lifted Barbara's cap down and slid it on her head, carefully tucking most of her hair into it. She happened to see herself in the mirror and, after deciding that she looked like a big white mushroom, made a face at her reflection and slowly descended into the bubbles.

The bubbles felt cool and the water felt hot. Lying in the tub, Claudia lifted her foot out of the water several times to test this interesting feeling. In the bubbles, she wiggled her big toe back and forth at herself. This reminded her of Janice and Polly wiggling up to her at the playground at school a few days ago to ask if she was coming to the party. Claudia had smiled sweetly and said that she would have to let Janice know, which she did at the very last minute on Friday afternoon. "I guess I'll be able to come to your party," she had said. Then she had heard Polly whisper excitedly, "Where do you suppose she got a . . ." And Janice had dug her in the ribs.

A loud banging on the bathroom door interrupted Claudia's thoughts.

"Hey, pest, I'm leaving. Good-bye!"

"David!" yelled Claudia. "You can't go yet! I'm in the tub."

"Look, sport, I'm late already. Paul's waiting for me to pick him up and we've got to get started."

"But you haven't even had breakfast!"

"We're going to eat on the way. Can't you stick your head out the door?"

"Gee whiz!" Claudia moaned. It wasn't fair. Although her mother usually had a terrible time getting

111

her into the tub, she had an even worse time getting her out again. Today, with no one bothering her, Claudia had planned to soak and soak. Mumbling to herself, she climbed out of the bubble-filled tub, threw on her terry bathrobe, opened the door a crack and peered around.

"You can't go, David. You just got here. We haven't done anything together. Nothing!"

"Claudia, I'm sorry. It's just the way things worked out. But, hey, I may be coming home the end of October for a few days. It's Claire's birthday."

Claudia stared at the floor, not able to say anything.

"Hey, pest, I'm not going to be spending every minute with her. Look, I'll make you a promise. One night, if Mom'll let you, we'll go out to dinner and a show. Will you buy that?"

"Just the two of us?" asked Claudia.

"Just the two of us."

Claudia grinned, then suddenly noticed that David was staring at her. She decided that she must look like a real creep with her face all pink and damp with wisps of hair sticking to her, and that huge mushroom on her head.

"What's wrong?" she asked.

"You know something, sport, some day you're going to be a knockout!" David reached out and rubbed his finger down her nose, then turned and ran down the stairs.

Claudia shut the door and then peered at her

steamed-up image in the mirror. "Now what kind of thing is that to say to a person?" she asked herself.

The fun of the bubble bath had ended, so Claudia dried herself and reached for the baby powder. Remembering something she had seen in the cabinet, she opened it and reached in there instead, pulling out the round box which held Barbara's bath powder. She carefully opened it and pulled out the fat lamb's-wool powder puff, basting herself liberally with it. Powder flew out all over the bathroom. Claudia knew it would take her at least twenty minutes to clear the tub of tell-tale bubbles, wipe off the powder from everything, and dry the shower cap, but she felt it had all been worthwhile.

For besides being a charm, this bath had turned into a kind of experiment. Bubble bath (perfumed). A shower cap (lace-trimmed). Fancy bath powder (applied with a lamb's-wool puff). Claudia wasn't sure whether she liked it or didn't like it. It was something a tomboy would have to think about.

At quarter to three that afternoon, wearing her new white blouse and plaid skirt, white knee socks, and brown loafers, Claudia was ready for the party. To the surprise of her mother, she was carrying her small corduroy zippered purse. Inside it she had hidden three lengths of broad Christmas ribbon, one green, one red, and one gold. It would have been difficult to explain to her mother why she needed the ribbon, so the only thing was to disguise it.

She waved good-bye and set off toward Janice's house, which was in the opposite direction from Duffy's house. Instead of crossing the street at the corner, however, she stopped to look back and see if her mother had gone into the house. Finding that she had, Claudia *turned* the corner and dashed around the block, finally coming right back down her own street. She ran up Duffy's driveway and saw with relief that Duffy's leg was hanging down through the branches of the apple tree.

"Hey, pssst, Duffy! I'm here!" she called out in a loud whisper.

Duffy climbed down from the tree in his usual careful way and approached the fence. "You made it!"

"Of course I made it!" Claudia said with an impatient toss of her head. "Is C. G. ready?" Caesar's Ghost, hearing his name, waved his tail wildly.

Duffy rubbed the dog's ear. "I brushed and combed him and sprayed him," he said.

"Phew! With what?"

"Violet water."

"It doesn't smell the same on dogs," Claudia said. "Anyway, here's a ribbon to tie on his collar." She handed Duffy a red Christmas ribbon from her purse. "Okay, let's get Prince and Bagel. Where's Leonie?" Claudia looked over toward the next yard and saw Leonie, Maurice, Robin, and Robby all leaning over the fence.

"I can come! I can come!" Leonie cried out.

"What did you tell your mother?" Claudia asked.

"I just asked if I could take Bagel for a walk. Then I told Mrs. Hennessey I was going for a walk with you and could we take Prince too. She said yes, so it's all right."

"Good," said Claudia. "Do Maurice and Robin and Robby all know this is a secret?" They all nodded. Maurice's eyes were so wide it looked as if the sides of them would split.

"Will you tell us again why we can't go?"

"Look, Maurice," Claudia said slowly and patiently, "a whole army doesn't go to every battle. Somebody has to stay back at the camp and guard it. Supposing we're all gone and the enemy comes up and *steals* something!" Maurice gasped and clutched the piece of rope he held tightly against his stomach. "Anyway," Claudia continued, "you and Robin and Robby can help tie this green ribbon on Prince's collar while Leonie goes to get Bagel." She and Duffy supervised this while Leonie brought Bagel from her own yard and tied the gold ribbon on him.

"Okay, hup, two, three, this way," Claudia said. "We can't go by my house." Duffy held C. G.'s leash, Leonie held Bagel's, and Claudia held Prince. With the excited dogs jumping all over them and each other, they set off in a direction away from Claudia's house. Not even daring to pass the other end of her block, Claudia made them detour around two extra blocks to get to Janice's house.

"Now, look," she said, "when we get there, you two will have to take all three dogs while I spy."

"Why can't you just go on in?" Duffy asked. "Are you going to change your mind?"

"Look, Duffy, nobody just walks into a battle without first checking the battlefield."

"I would," Duffy said. "Otherwise I'd probably never get there."

"We'd better do what Claudia says," Leonie said.

"Oh, I will," said Duffy. "Where are we going to hide with three dogs, though?"

"There's this tall hedge all around Janice's house," Claudia replied. "All you and Leonie have to do is stand outside it while I creep around to the back where the party is. Then if it's all right, I'll come back for the dogs. Get it?"

"Got it," said Duffy. Leonie, wide-eyed, nodded.

"See, here's the hedge," Claudia announced when they had arrived at Janice's house. "Now you wait here and I'll be right back." She handed Prince's leash to Duffy and then left, sneaking along close to the tall hedge. As she neared the back garden, she could hear music mixed with the murmur of girls' voices.

The party had already started, which was what Claudia had planned and expected. After all, it would have been no use at all to spy on an empty battlefield. She put her nose up to the hedge and peered in. If the hedge had not been so dense, she might very well have hurtled right through it trying to get a closer look at what was before her.

Claudia counted six girls, including Janice and Polly, sitting around in garden chairs. They were dressed not only in party dresses — Claudia groaned — but in stockings and shoes with little heels on them. All six girls were holding tiny dogs. Four of the dogs were toy poodles, one was a chihuahua, and one something with hair over its eyes. Claudia couldn't tell what *it* was.

All the dogs wore jewelled collars and Janice's and Polly's dogs had matching ribbons tied into bows on their heads. Claudia congratulated herself on having brought Christmas ribbons for *her* dogs.

Claudia recognized but didn't actually know any of the other girls. One, a seventh-grader, was a friend of Polly's. Two others were seventh-graders, too, and one was an eighth-grader.

Claudia poked her nose further into the hedge, looking now at a table behind the girls. The table was draped in a lace tablecloth and decorated with a vase of yellow chrysanthemums. Each place was set with a paper cup bearing the picture of a dog, and also with a tiny bone tied with a yellow ribbon. A large platter on the table seemed to hold more bones, until Claudia decided that these must be cookies.

She drew back a little as Janice rose from her chair. "I just *do* believe we'll have to start without her."

Polly smirked. "Oh, do you really think we *should?*"

"Well, she's *terribly* late, you know." Claudia told herself it couldn't be much more than three minutes past three. "I guess we simply *will* have to start. Polly, I hope you'll pour?"

Pour? Pour what? Claudia asked herself. Were they

going to have tea and coffee? Janice must be losing her mind. Claudia watched, fascinated, as the girls clustered around the table.

"Oh, Janice, how sweet!"

"Isn't this darling?"

"Precious!"

Claudia, nearly hypnotized, decided that she had better be on her way. Hugging the hedge, she raced back to where Duffy and Leonie waited with the dogs.

"Okay, I'll take them now," she said as she grabbed the leashes.

"Should we wait here for you, Claudia?" Duffy asked.

"I don't know how long I'll be," she replied.

"Oh, you probably won't be too long," said Duffy. "We'll wait."

Remembering the dainty girls hugging their almost invisible dogs gave Claudia the feeling that she wouldn't be very long, either. "All right," she said, "but if I'm . . ." Claudia couldn't finish her sentence.

The three dogs, suddenly overwhelmed by the scent of the tea party for pets, gave a tremendous tug on their leashes and careened off toward the back of the house, Claudia flying along behind them.

Claudia had considered announcing herself over the back gate, but the gate, as it turned out, was not properly latched. The dogs simply pushed on it with their paws and bounded in, lunging toward the tea table and the small dogs in the arms of their mistresses.

Claudia, lurching in behind them, felt the leashes slip from her hands.

The girls began to shriek hysterically. "Claudia! What are you doing? Take those dogs away!" Janice screamed.

The sound of Janice's voice seemed to please Bagel, because he immediately put his huge paws up on her shoulders and started to lick her face. She squealed and clutched La Petite to her breast, from which vantage point the small dog peered out, panting — clearly delighted with Bagel's slobbering attention.

"Help! Help!" yelled Janice. No one paid much attention to her, however, because Prince, hopelessly excited, had begun to bark fiercely at the other girls and they had all climbed up on chairs. This made Prince even more distraught, and he ran around in circles, stopping at one chair and then another, pawing the ground, barking, and generally acting like a lunatic.

While this was going on, Caesar's Ghost galloped to the table where, with paws right in the center of the lace tablecloth, he was happily helping himself to bones, cookies, and anything else he could find.

Claudia simply stood and stared, completely immobilized by the enormity of the mess she had created and by the fact that she really couldn't decide which dog to capture first. Janice decided for her by roaring, "Claudia, you take this dog off me or I'll . . ." and she grabbed Bagel's leash.

Janice's face was flushed and furious. "Look, Claudia, how dare you! Who said you could bring these . . . these *animals* to my party?"

"You did!" cried Claudia. "You said in your invitation I had to bring a dog!"

"Well, I didn't tell you to bring *three* dogs!"

"You didn't tell me *not* to!"

Janice wobbled on her high heels. She looked as if she might be going to hit Claudia. "Well . . . well . . . well, they aren't even *your* dogs!"

"They are too! They're mine for the afternoon!" By now, Claudia and Janice were screaming at each other, and their voices rose over the barking of the dogs. The other girls stared at them.

Caesar's Ghost chose that moment to descend from the table, dragging the lace tablecloth with him. Everything on the table — cups, bones, cookies, flowers, everything — came crashing to the ground. Both Prince and Bagel headed for the feast while all the small dogs struggled frantically in the arms of their owners.

Janice had looked as if she were about to cry at any moment and now, at last, tears ran down her face. "Mo-o-o-ther!" she wailed. "Mo-o-o-ther!"

Claudia didn't know why Mrs. Irby hadn't already appeared, but in any event, she now paddled out from the house, her little hands waving helplessly around in the air like the fronds of a distracted sea anemone.

"M-m-m-mother!" sobbed Janice. "She's ruined my party. M-m-m-make her go home!"

"Who, dear?" asked Mrs. Irby.

"Claudia!" Janice moaned. "And make her take these dogs away."

"Oh dear, I'm sure she didn't mean to. It must have been all a mistake. Oh dear, Claudia, perhaps you'd better go." Mrs. Irby picked up a smashed paper cup and stared bleakly at it.

Claudia had by now managed to gather the dogs together and the girls were starting to climb down from the chairs as she approached the gate. Everyone simply stared silently at her as she left, dragging the reluctant dogs after her.

Claudia wondered if she herself were going to cry, but she knew she couldn't allow herself to break down. She had to face Duffy and Leonie, and arriving in tears would have suggested that the battle had been lost and the army was routed. She was not really sure what the outcome of the battle was, because she had never been sure what she was setting out to accomplish in the first place. But if it had been lost, it would never do to admit it to the rest of the army.

Anyway, the dogs had had a good time.

Eleven

IT WAS SUNDAY AFTERNOON and Claudia was lying on the living-room floor with her feet up on the couch, reading her favorite story about horses, when the telephone rang. She heard her mother answer it and then, satisfied that the call wasn't for her (though who would be calling her, anyway, she had no idea), she retreated immediately into her book. Then all at once it sounded as if the call might have something to do with her after all. She glanced secretly at her father and saw that he was deeply engrossed in the Sunday paper. Still, not wanting to get a lecture on eavesdropping, Claudia pretended to keep on reading, all the while listening to her mother so hard that her ears almost hurt.

"Why, no, Clara, she didn't tell me anything about

your sending her home from the party." (Claudia had played in the forest for an hour after bringing the dogs home.) "No, you certainly don't need to apologize." (Apologize? For what?) "*Three* dogs!" (Oh, oh! thought Claudia.) "No, indeed, Clara, I'm sure she did *not* misunderstand the invitation. . . . Of course, that's what I told her. . . . Well, as far as I knew, she didn't have any dogs with her when she left the house. . . . You're very kind, but I'll certainly have something to say to her about this. . . ."

Claudia put down her book quietly, rose, and headed for the door. "Just a minute, young lady!" said her father. He was cheating. He had been listening all along. Claudia stopped in the doorway, her back stiff. Then she turned and walked slowly back into the living room.

"That was Mrs. Irby!" announced Mrs. Harper, coming in behind her.

Claudia faced her mother, clamping her lips together in a tight line, just as she used to do when she was very small and her mother tried to force a spoonful of baby carrots into her mouth.

"Well, aren't you going to say anything?"

"What would you like me to say?" asked Claudia, opening her mouth just enough to squeeze the words through.

"Look here, Claudia," said Mr. Harper, putting the paper down on the floor with a crackling thump, "I don't want to hear that tone of voice. Now your mother clearly wants an explanation for something

123

you did, though heaven only knows what it was, and I want you to give it to her . . . *politely!*"

"What Claudia did," Mrs. Harper interrupted, "was to attend Janice Irby's party with *three* dogs. She ruined the party . . . spoiled it completely. And that pleasant Clara Irby was nice enough to apologize for having to send Claudia home. Oh!" Mrs. Harper threw up her hands and raised her eyes to the ceiling.

A curious look crossed Mr. Harper's face. "Where on earth did she get three dogs?"

"She took those three neighborhood hoodlums, Bagel, Prince, and Caesar's Ghost, naturally!"

"They're not hoodlums!" yelled Claudia.

"Now don't you change the subject!" her father warned her. "See here, young lady, I think you had better march right up to your room and stay there for the rest of the day. As a matter of fact, change that to the rest of the week. Except for school, you are hereby confined to quarters this whole coming week."

"It's not fair!" Claudia burst out, shaking her head so that her hair sprayed across her eyes. She put out her lower lip and blew the hair angrily away. "I just did what the invitation said. It said I had to take a dog. And it never said I couldn't take three. Three is better than one, isn't it?" Claudia wished she could have thought of something to say that made more sense.

"That is enough!" said her father with the kind of look Claudia knew better than to argue with. "Now go!"

Claudia marched noisily up the stairs. Halfway up she stopped. There was absolute silence in the living room. Then she heard her mother say, "Well, what are you grinning about? I don't see anything funny about this."

Claudia kept her feet on the same step, but she slid her hands down the bannister so far, to get her ears nearer the living room, that if her parents should have surprised her by suddenly appearing, she would have fallen flat on her face.

"I just happened to think," said her father, "that . . . uh . . . taking three dogs to the party was, well, enterprising, to say the least."

"You *would* think it was something like that. *I* don't think it was even . . . well . . . civilized. I mean, Janice was nice enough to send her an invitation to a party. . . ."

"Great Scott, Fran, it was a kind of backhanded invitation. You have to admit that."

"Yes, I suppose it was. I wish I knew what was going on between Janice and Claudia."

"Whatever it is, it'll blow over."

"I don't know. I thought when we put an end to Duffy that things like this wouldn't keep happening."

An interesting silence followed. Then Claudia heard her father clearing his throat.

"Ah . . . you're not considering allowing Claudia to start playing with Duffy again, are you?"

At this Claudia nearly let go of the bannister.

"I should say not! Anyway, Duffy wasn't entirely

125

uninvolved in this latest . . . enterprise as you put it. One of the dogs was *his*, you know. And for heaven's sake, stop grinning. Oh, go back to your paper! I'm going out and finish putting the roast in the oven."

Claudia regained her balance and tiptoed quickly on up the steps and into her room. With things so pleasant once again in the living room, she very nearly lost her head and went back down. She caught herself in time, however, fortunately remembering the misery this dangerous kind of thinking had caused her in the past. At the sight of her face, her parents would get mad all over again, possibly to the point of increasing her punishment.

Claudia sniffed as she dropped into her desk chair and opened her book. At least she had remembered to bring her book. Well, if she was going to have to spend the rest of the day in her room, she would certainly need that!

When Claudia entered her classroom on Monday morning, neither Janice nor Polly so much as looked at her. They simply stared stonily ahead when she walked by. It was about what Claudia expected.

The day started with Mrs. Aiken announcing that they were going to elect class officers the following week. "By then you should have had lots of time to get acquainted with one another. You can all be thinking about people you would like to nominate," she said.

Claudia wondered if there was anyone *she* would like to nominate. Sarah? No, she had already told herself that she was no longer going to worry about Sarah. She even wondered why she had wanted to be friends with Sarah. Wheat germ! What was *that* to be friends about?

Jack Sherwood? Somebody else would probably nominate him.

No, Claudia told herself, she guessed she wouldn't nominate anyone. Nevertheless, along with the rest of the class, she peered at everyone as if she were seriously considering each one as a candidate.

Almost as soon as class got under way, the notes started streaming between Janice's and Polly's desks. Claudia felt that she knew what ninety percent of the notes were about. Still, this only made her more curious to see one. She did, at last, shortly after art period.

Claudia could always tell when Mr. Dalroy came into the room because Janice's neck would turn pink. It was like watching the sunrise, really fascinating. Nearly all the girls in the sixth grade were in love with Mr. Dalroy, but Claudia felt that Janice and Polly were losing their minds over it. She could imagine what they were thinking when Mr. Dalroy announced that in three or four weeks he was going to select several sixth-grade art students to work with him on preparing sets for the P.T.A. Christmas show. Janice's neck turned crimson and Polly's eyes popped so far out that it looked as if they might fall out of her head

127

and roll down the aisle like two blue marbles. There would be no living with either of them if they were selected.

At the end of the art period, Mr. Dalroy had another announcement that seemed to throw the two girls into a frenzy. Some of his art supplies were missing, he told the class, and he asked that each person check his desk to make sure nothing had found its way there by mistake. He said, too, that his gold watch had been lost, politely suggesting, Claudia supposed, that it might also have found its way into someone's desk. Everyone immediately dove into his own desk and came up shaking his head. Janice and Polly added sweet smiles to their head-shakes and then blushed furiously when Mr. Dalroy smiled back at them in a kind of distracted way.

Mr. Dalroy had no sooner left the room at the end of the period than Claudia saw a note leave Janice's desk and snake its way across the floor. It was unseen by Mrs. Aiken, who was returning to the classroom. Before Polly could even lean over to get it, Claudia reached out her foot and grabbed it. As she drew her foot back with the note safely under it, Janice turned around and threw her a look of rage. "You give that back!" she hissed.

Claudia held the note under her desk and smiled innocently. Then, while Janice ripped a piece of paper from her notebook and scribbled angrily on it, Claudia unfolded the note and read it. Janice had drawn a large heart and in it enclosed the words, "Janice Irby and Robby Dalroy." (Robby? This *killed* Claudia. She choked back a giggle.) Under the heart Janice had written, "Isn't he darling? Poor thing. I wonder who stole his watch?"

Stole? Who said anything about stealing anything? Wasn't it just like Janice to think of *that!* Claudia folded the note up again and slipped it into her skirt pocket just as another note was delivered to her from under Janice's arm. "You'd better give it back or you'll be sorry!"

Claudia read this and then ripped up the note right under Janice's ear. Janice whirled around and said, "Don't you . . ."

"Girls! You are supposed to be studying your history. Did I see someone pass a note?" How were *they* supposed to know if she saw someone pass a note! Nobody answered Mrs. Aiken's question.

Mrs. Aiken didn't appear angry, only in pain. Claudia thought her ulcer must be killing her. In any event, Mrs. Aiken was in no mood for further interruptions, so when Itty Bitty raised his hand and announced that he didn't feel well, Mrs. Aiken told him that he looked fine and to go back to his work. Claudia saw Itty's face slowly turn to sea green and finally to no color at all. Then, without asking permission, Itty rose from his desk and lunged into the hall. They could hear him throwing up all the way to the boys' room. Mrs. Aiken started up after him and then, looking green herself, sat down again and asked Jack Sherwood to please get the janitor. Bobby Paine started to make loud choking, gagging sounds but nobody thought he was very funny and someone told him to shut up. He stopped immediately, embarrassed and mad.

With all this, nothing further happened with the note. Claudia considered the possibility of handing it back to Janice if she should ask for it again, but at the noon bell, Janice only looked at her coldly and marched out with Polly.

Janice and Polly usually sat in a cozy group of two off by themselves somewhere, but today Claudia saw them approach a table filled with Mrs. Aiken's sixth-grade girls. All through lunch, the girls at that table kept their heads in close formation while Janice and Polly appeared to be giving out what looked like foot-ball signals. Claudia would have dismissed the whole matter from her mind, except that from time to time the girls all turned as if they were one big wind-up toy and stared at her. Then, after lunch, she forgot about the whole lunch table mystery in a wild game of kick-ball with the boys.

As for the note, that subject never came up again because Janice wouldn't talk to Claudia at all. Except for the fact that Claudia knew it was hidden in her small Chinese chest at home, together with her other secret papers, the incident might never have hap-pened at all.

Twelve

Mrs. Harper was transferring some cold leftover soup from a larger to a smaller bowl the next morning while the rest of the family ate breakfast.

"That's the way Itty sounded," announced Claudia.

"That's the way Itty sounded doing what, dear?" inquired her mother.

"Throwing up," replied Claudia, calmly sipping her orange juice.

"Oh, honestly! Make her stop it! What next! She'll ruin our breakfast!"

"Barbara's right, dear," said Mrs. Harper. "That isn't exactly table conversation."

"Well, I don't care," Claudia shot back, more at Barbara than at her mother. "That's the way throwing up sounds in our school hall."

Mr. Harper set down his coffee cup. "Claudia, that is enough! We're not interested in either Itty or the way he . . . sounds in the school hall. Now, if you don't mind, the subject is closed."

Claudia retreated into gloomy silence. So many of her conversations with her family ended this way, by her being told to keep quiet or change the subject. At least it seemed that way at the moment. What was wrong with talking about somebody being sick? If she and Duffy had been on the subject, they would have had a very interesting conversation about it. In any event, Claudia left for school feeling cross and miserable.

The conversation was a bad beginning to a bad day. Claudia wondered later if that was what it was, or if she had forgotten to rub her finger around the newel post three times when she forgot a book and had to go back after it.

A group of sixth-grade girls were clustered at the front door of the school when Claudia arrived. They looked at her with expressionless faces as she approached them, and then they turned their backs toward her. Claudia looked closer to see if Janice and Polly might be part of the group, but she could see that they weren't. She decided that she was imagining things and continued toward the girls. Without a word to her, but with several significant glances toward each other, the girls all began to drift away, leaving Claudia standing on the school steps alone.

She told herself firmly that she was not going to cry, and then pinched herself hard to make sure that she didn't. She wondered if she should go to the girls' room until she felt better, but finally decided against it. She knew she would cry in the girls' room and, if she stayed there long enough, someone would be sent to find her. She would have to walk into the classroom looking like a wet, red-eyed rabbit.

What Claudia finally did do was run to the rings and swing herself across and back three times. It kept her from thinking about crying and she could enter the school building without making a spectacle of herself.

She found another group meeting in the classroom, this one headed by Janice Irby and Polly McKisson. "Sh-sh-sh, here she comes!" someone hissed when Claudia appeared. After a good deal of nudging and several dark glances at Claudia, the group dissolved, melting away to individual desks in the best tradition of seasoned sixth-grade secret agents. Claudia felt like public school enemy number one.

For whatever it was worth, and that was not much at the moment, Sarah What's-her-name (Sarah's last name was Carvell but Claudia wouldn't admit that she cared what it was) had not been part of the meeting. She sat at her desk paying no attention to it and was, as usual, scribbling in her drawing tablet. She didn't even look up when Claudia came in.

Itty's desk was empty. Claudia hoped that whatever Itty had was catching and that, excluding herself, the whole class would get it, especially Janice and Polly. The disease might even turn out to be fatal. She stopped thinking this, however, when it occurred to her that it meant Itty would also have to die. She was miserable enough without thinking of Itty on his deathbed.

Things were no better at lunchtime. Claudia had always managed to find an empty seat at one of Mrs. Aiken's sixth-grade tables in the cafeteria, but today when she headed for one, someone next to it pulled the chair away from the table and shoved it into the middle of the floor. Then she saw another empty place next to Alice Clay and headed for that. Alice quickly slid into the empty chair and advised Claudia in a frosty voice that she was saving it for a friend. Claudia finally ended up at a fifth-grade table. Her throat felt so tight that she had to swallow three times to get one bite of peanut-butter sandwich down.

Claudia didn't feel like braving the playground after that, so she returned to the classroom and sat staring out the window until the bell rang. Holy tomato! Holy tomato! She said that over and over again to keep herself from crying. Suddenly life had become one big round of finding things to do or say to keep from crying. Oh, holy tomato, anyway! Claudia took a big jab at her desk with her pencil, but all she did was break the lead.

Unfortunately, they had Miss Murdock that afternoon. Claudia was in no mood for Miss Murdock. Oddly enough, though, she didn't mind doing the warm-up exercises and even wished they would spend the whole time doing them. But Miss Murdock, eyeing them critically while they collapsed into their deep knee bends, told them that their leg muscles were completely out of shape. Tired legs, she called it. And it just so happened that she, Miss Murdock, had thought up a splendid game for putting the snap in their worn-out elastic. "The game," she said, "is called 'toad and frogs.'"

Even before hearing the rules, Claudia knew it was a terrible game. Any game with a name like that would have to be terrible.

"Now," continued Miss Murdock, "this is a game which is played in exactly the same manner as tag. The toad is 'it' and chases the frogs, except we will all get down on our hands and hop, hop, hop about as if we were a real little toad and real little frogs. Like this . . ." She reached down to the ground and started leaping in one direction and then another, her whistle swinging madly about. Hop, hop, hop. Back and forth, around and around she went, looking less and less like a frog and more and more like a deranged hippopotamus with every leap.

All at once, almost by accident it seemed, she looked up at the girls. A startled look crossed her face and she turned a bright crimson. Then she stood up quickly and blew a sharp fweep on her whistle as if it were the *girls* who had been behaving like lunatics.

"Now, is there anyone who doesn't understand how it's done?" she said briskly.

Claudia thought she might raise her hand and ask Miss Murdock to do it again, but then she decided she didn't feel like it. She didn't really feel like doing anything. All she wanted was to go home.

"Let me see," said Miss Murdock, "whom shall we have for our first toad?" The girls all looked around, considering each other's toadlike qualities.

Janice Irby raised her hand. "I have a good idea for a toad," she said. "I think Claudia Harper would make a good toad." Several of Mrs. Aiken's sixth-grade girls snickered.

"Splendid! A splendid suggestion!" said Miss Murdock, beaming at Claudia.

Claudia felt hot down through her toenails.

"Hop, frogs, hop! Chase, toad, chase!" sang Miss Murdock. Down went all the girls on their hands and off they hopped. Claudia, down on her hands, hopped after them.

She knew that she looked like an idiot, and the thought that they all looked like idiots didn't make her feel any better. The last thing she wanted to do at the moment was go leaping all over the playground, chasing people.

"Toad! Toad! Toad! You nasty old toad!" screamed Mrs. Aiken's sixth-grade girls, and the others picked up the chant. They stayed together in groups taunting Claudia until she hopped over, then they all broke up, chortling and screeching.

Ordinarily, Claudia would have loved being the toad. She liked being "it" in any game. But today her legs felt like melting rubber. It hurt to breathe and her eyes weren't focusing. The bunched-up girls would burst apart like bubbles in a witch's cauldron, leaving Claudia hopelessly flopping around after nothing, then always managing to choose the wrong person to chase. When the bell rang, Claudia hadn't caught anyone and was still the toad. All the way back to the classroom, the girls were snickering and staring, and whispering, "Toad! Toad!" in her direction. If she *had* been a toad, Claudia told herself, she would have squirted her poison juice all over them.

Nothing got much better after that day. The hardest part was not knowing why she had suddenly become the class creep. Claudia started thinking a lot about the kids she had considered class creeps in the past. There was, for instance, Amos Early in the fourth grade. Amos rarely took baths. He told someone once that water made his skin break out all over in purple warts. Nobody believed him, though, because who ever heard of water making your skin break out in purple warts? Claudia began to wonder if she smelled bad the way Amos did. She smelled herself secretly but then decided that *that* didn't do any good. You get so used to the way you smell, she told herself, that even if it was bad, you could never tell it. Look at skunks, for instance. But just in case, she started scrubbing herself so hard in her bath that her skin smarted and turned red.

Claudia found out, too, how it felt to be the last one chosen in sports. She had always known that it was terrible, but it turned out to be worse than terrible. She wondered how Sarah had lived through it all these years. Claudia made up her mind that if she ever had a turn at being team captain again, she was going to choose some people like Sarah first. So what if your team *did* lose! It was terrible to be chosen last.

But the worst thing that happened, though, was the class election.

The only person who ever smiled at Claudia was Itty, and even he did it quickly, as if he might be caught and get killed. Claudia nearly died herself when Itty actually raised his hand and nominated her for vice-president on the day of the election. His face was white when he did it, and his hand looked, going up, as if it were about to dive into a pot of hot grease. Itty stared straight ahead at the blackboard and the rest of the class was so still you could hear people breathing.

Unfortunately, Mrs. Aiken did not believe in sending people out of the room during the voting. Just before it was time to vote for vice-president, Bobby Paine leaned over and socked Itty on the arm because he was still staring at the blackboard and refused to look around when Bobby cleared his throat and coughed about ten times. The sock on the arm must have impressed Itty, because when Claudia's name was called out, he continued to stare at the blackboard but didn't raise his hand. Claudia got one vote and that was her own. Even that was because she put her hand up by accident and then was too proud to pull it down when someone snickered.

That was the worst thing that happened.

Claudia felt at times as if she wanted to jump up and scream, "I'm not it!" or "I didn't do it!" But not *what?* Or didn't *do* what? How can you say you're not something or didn't do something if you don't even know what you're talking about? It would be like going up to some policeman and saying, "Look, I didn't do it!" You would get arrested for just *saying* it.

Once Claudia was so desperate that she even considered discussing the situation with her family, her mother, her father, or even Barbara. But she couldn't. She found that she couldn't say anything at all about it at home. All she did was cry without being able to explain why she was crying.

One morning at breakfast, Barbara raised her nose in the air and started sniffing. "Phew! What's *that?*" Claudia had just walked into the room.

"I don't know," Mr. Harper said, "but I rather like it."

Claudia sat down at the table, saying nothing. She had just helped herself to her father's shaving lotion in case her bath the night before hadn't been enough.

Barbara kept on sniffing. "Claudia, what have you done to yourself? You smell."

This was too much and Claudia burst into tears right there at the table.

"Look here, Barbara . . ." Mr. Harper began.

"I'm sorry. I didn't mean anything. It's just that she's got something on that smells, that's all."

"That is enough, Barbara!"

"I said I was sorry."

"It's all right, Barbara, I'm sure Claudia accepts your apology," said Mrs. Harper, putting her arm around Claudia and giving her a hug. "There, there, dear, Barbara didn't mean anything. Here, let me look at you." She raised Claudia's wet face and looked anxiously at one side and then the other. "Claudia, you feel all right, don't you? Are you feeling all right?" She put her hand on Claudia's forehead. "Dear, is anything the matter?"

Claudia shook her head and blew her nose into her paper napkin. The napkin scratched and made her eyes smart.

"I don't know. I wonder." Mrs. Harper sounded even more worried. "You know we never did have Dr. Bauman check you over before school this year. Maybe I'd better call him and make an appointment. Would you like that, dear?"

Claudia burst out sobbing again.

Her mother patted her on the head. "All right, dear, we won't make an appointment just yet."

"Look, Fran," Mr. Harper offered from behind his

cup of coffee. "She'll be all right. She probably just had too much of her room last week. It'll blow over."

Her mother wanting to take her to the doctor. Her father saying it would all blow over. It was all more than Claudia could bear. Gasping and sobbing, she pushed her chair back and raced up to her room. Her mother followed her up, of course, and it all ended by Claudia climbing back into her pajamas and returning to bed. She happened to be wearing her favorite green pajamas with the goofy black whales all over them, but even that wasn't as comforting as it usually was.

Claudia hoped she would never burst into tears like that again. But she did.

Once was simply because her mother said one night that they were out of peanut butter and her father said he was too tired to go to the store for some. And Claudia had other crying spells that seemed just as pointless.

Mr. Harper kept right on saying that it would blow over. Mrs. Harper kept right on talking about going to the doctor, only they never went. And Claudia even overheard Barbara telling her mother that it was just Claudia's age, whatever that meant.

Claudia actually did get sick once and was spared a whole week of school. She came down with flu. Everyone at home was so nice, and in a way this made her feel even worse, because no one knew that they were being nice to someone who was this big creep at school. Still, Claudia knew that it pleased her mother to have something definite to work with, and she let herself be fed Jello and have her temperature taken a thousand times a day without complaining once.

In any event, now everyone was certain that Claudia's problem was that she had been coming down with the flu. Anything that happened later would be because she hadn't gotten over it yet.

The flu bug had solved everything for everyone but Claudia.

Thirteen

"I LIKE IT. It's what I want to wear exactly."

"It's all right, dear, but I wish you could have picked something more . . . more . . . well, it just isn't the kind of thing most *girls* would want to wear."

Claudia and her mother were talking about Claudia's Halloween costume. Claudia was wearing a pair of David's old trousers stuffed with a pillow and tied up with rope. This was topped by the jacket her father had worn when he was in the army. On her head she wore his officer's cap, which came down over her ears. She had to tilt her head way back to even see out from under it.

She strutted around in front of the mirror, saluting herself and clicking her heels, then tipping her head back so she could have a better look at the mustache she had applied with her mother's eyebrow pencil. Her mother was laughing at her, but in a kind of worried and horrified way. Claudia knew her mother would have been much happier if she was going out as a fairy or a princess, or even a witch. Something about her being in an army uniform really bothered everyone.

Actually, Claudia hadn't planned to go out on Halloween at all this year. Then Mrs. Friedman telephoned and asked if Claudia *was* going and would she take Leonie and Maurice along with her. Mrs. Harper had said that Claudia would be glad to and then had telephoned Mrs. Hennessey to suggest that Robin and Robby go along too.

It was Maurice who had given Claudia the idea of wearing the army uniform when he asked if this couldn't be an expedition of the secret army where they could go and spy on the enemy. Maurice had never recovered from missing the dog party. He was so disappointed at having stayed at home to guard the camp and then having nobody come to attack it or steal something.

Spying on Janice and Polly began to sound like a very good idea to Claudia. Although she didn't know why she had become the class creep, she would have been pretty stupid not to have known who started it. Claudia had been so miserable that she had almost forgotten the idea of spying at school or any place else. She was glad that Maurice had thought about spying on Halloween. It wouldn't accomplish much, but it was like having the poison paper in her little Chinese chest — a secret, comforting thing to do.

Leonie, Maurice, Robin, and Robby were all waiting for Claudia on the Friedmans' front lawn when she left her house. So was Duffy. Nothing had been said about Duffy going with them and Claudia hadn't mentioned it. Her parents must know that he would be with the rest of the children. Or did they? Claudia didn't want to give them the chance to say no by asking.

"Gee, Duffy, what are *you* supposed to be?" was what Claudia said when she saw him.

"A washing machine," replied Duffy. "See, this is where you load me up." He opened a round, cellophane-covered flap at about the place where his stomach was.

A washing machine! That certainly sounded like Duffy.

"Holy tomato, Duffy!" Claudia said happily.

"I'm a monster! I'm a monster! Hey, look, Claudia, I'm a scary monster!" Robby yelled. He was wearing a dime store costume complete with fanged and bleeding monster's mask.

Robin hopped wildly around. "And I'm a bunny rabbit! See Claudia?"

Maurice, no longer able to control himself, burst in with, "And I'm a Christmas shepherd, Claudia. I came early. See, this is my crook." He waved a long broom handle under Claudia's nose. Maurice was wearing a striped bathrobe and had a white cloth on his head secured by his old piece of rope. Claudia whistled admiringly at him. She didn't think anything about Maurice being a Christmas shepherd because both Leonie and Maurice were allowed to sing Christmas carols with her around the neighborhood each year. Their parents allowed them even though they didn't get to have a Christmas tree or anything like that. Claudia thought it was nice that they were allowed to sing carols.

Leonie smiled shyly at her. "I'm something Christmas, too, Claudia. I'm a Christmas angel."

"Gee, Leonie," Claudia told her. "You look beautiful."

"Hey, Claudia, what are you?" Duffy asked.

"What does it look like? I'm an army officer," said Claudia. "Didn't Leonie tell you we were going spying tonight?"

"I wish I was an army officer," said Maurice.

"Look, Maurice, being a Christmas shepherd is a lot better than being an old army officer. Nobody's going to think a Christmas shepherd is a spy, so you can spy a whole lot better," Claudia said. This satisfied Maurice.

Everyone was carrying a small paper sack except for Claudia who was holding an oversized grocery bag. "Are you expecting to get all that filled?" Duffy asked.

Claudia looked sideways toward her house before replying. "No. See, I've got a small bag inside. I had to use this big one to get these out of the house." She reached in and pulled out the two cloth dolls from her sister's room.

Maurice gasped.

"What are we going to do with those?" asked Leonie.

"It's a kind of black magic," Claudia said. "See, one of these dolls is Janice and one of them is Polly. . . ."

"Which one?" asked Maurice.

"It doesn't matter which one. The thing is we're going to take them with us so that our spying will work out. Robin and Robby, you can hold them." Claudia had tied cords around the dolls' necks which the children held. The dolls looked as if they had been hanged.

Maurice hung his head and began to rub his eyes.

"Look, Maurice, we'll take turns," Claudia said quickly. "Now, if everyone is ready, we'll go." She looked at each one, grinning when she came to Duffy. "Jeepers, Duffy! Who ever heard of anyone being a washing machine for Halloween?"

Duffy beamed and waddled over so he could walk with her at the head of the line.

Claudia was glad she had come after all. She loved seeing the lighted pumpkins on the front porches and the skeletons hanging in the windows. The people in their neighborhood were all nice to kids on Halloween and made a big fuss over their costumes. It was too much fun to miss.

They went to a lot of the houses, but they missed some, too, because the army seemed to be anxious to get to Janice's house to spy. Especially Maurice.

It was not until they approached the house and saw the Irbys' lighted pumpkin on the front porch that Claudia began to wonder if this was all such a good idea after all. Knowing her, something would have to go wrong, and she was in enough mess as it was right now. By the time they got to the house, she knew it was not a good idea, so she lined them all up in front

"Look, army," she said, "instead of spying, I've decided that what we're going to do is just stand out here and put a black magic spell on the house. I've decided that's best."

"I want to spy," Maurice said.

"Look, Maurice, we can't."

"I want to spy," said Maurice again, and before Claudia could stop him, he had grabbed a doll from Robin and started with it toward the house. "They won't catch me. I'm a Christmas shepherd and you said I could spy a lot better."

"You get back here!" Claudia hissed as she started after him.

She was too late. Before she could get to him, he had already gone up to the living-room window, pressed his nose up against it, and started waving the doll over his head. The Irby front door swung open and Mrs. Irby's anxious face peered out.

"Why it's Claudia Harper and her little friends! Come to the door, Janice. It's Claudia!"

Claudia groaned. She had looked through the living room window just long enough to see Janice and Polly McKisson sitting there watching television together. They weren't even in costumes but were wearing dresses and stockings and their silly little high heels. Janice and Polly both appeared at the front door withMrs. Irby.

"It's Claudia, dear," Mrs. Irby went on. "Isn't this nice? Claudia, you must bring your little friends in and have Janice and Polly serve you some apple cider and cookies."

"Oh, we really can't, Mrs. Irby," Claudia said. "We still have lots of places to go."

"Nonsense! You must come in for just a minute and let us see your nice costumes!"

"We don't have lots of places to go," said Maurice.

"I want some cookies," Robby said.

"There, you see?" burbled Mrs. Irby. "Now, come right in children. You know," she murmured confidentially to Claudia, "the girls just didn't want to go out this Halloween. They're such little ladies now." Claudia thought she was going to be sick right on the spot.

They all went into the living room. "You just sit down and be comfortable, children, while Janice and

Polly serve you. Janice made the cookies herself, Claudia. Isn't that nice? Now, I'm going to leave because we don't need any grown-ups around, do we?" Mrs. Irby drifted gaily out.

Janice and Polly went to the kitchen and returned with a tray full of little cider-filled paper cups and a plate of cookies. So far, neither one had said a word to Claudia.

Janice looked at Duffy, who had had to remain standing because he couldn't bend in the middle enough to sit down. "What are you supposed to be?"

"A washing machine," said Duffy, chewing on a mouthful of cookie.

Janice and Polly looked at one another and snickered.

"What are you?" Janice asked Maurice next.

"A Christmas shepherd," Maurice said proudly.

"What's that doll you're holding?" Polly asked.

Maurice began to wave the doll back and forth. "It's my black magic doll. It's my turn to hold him. Claudia says . . ."

"Look, Maurice," Claudia burst in, nearly choking on her apple cider, "never mind about the doll. You just hold it . . . okay?"

Janice flicked her eyebrows at Polly. "And what are you?" she asked Leonie.

"I'm a Christmas angel," Leonie replied, smiling at Claudia.

"A Christmas angel?" Janice said, her voice rising. "Aren't you the Friedman children?"

Leonie nodded.

"What are you doing being a Christmas angel, then?" Instead of looking at Leonie, Janice was actually staring defiantly at Claudia.

Leonie said nothing for a moment. "I don't know," she said at last and hung her head.

Claudia wanted to hit Janice, to smack her right across her big mouth.

"Look, Janice, Leonie can be a Christmas angel if she wants to!" Claudia tried to keep her voice down but it was hard not to scream at Janice's big, fat head.

"I wasn't asking *you*," Janice said. "I just *really* don't see how she can be a Christmas angel, that's all."

Claudia stood up and marched over to her. "I'll tell you how she can be a Christmas angel. I'll tell you!" Claudia was starting to bellow. "It's because God never said she *couldn't*, that's why. God never said anybody could or couldn't be a Christmas angel. I'll bet God is glad to get all the Christmas angels he can get and I'll bet Leonie is one of the best ones he has. So you just shut up, Janice Irby!" It was terrible to be using words like shut up when you were talking about God, but Claudia was too mad to worry about it.

Janice sniffed and then carefully reviewed Claudia from the top of her father's cap to the cuffs of her brother's tied-on trousers. "Well! I don't see how people who wear . . . *men's* clothes like that and bust up other people's parties and STEAL know so much about God. I *really* don't!"

"What do you mean, *steal?*" Claudia shot back. She glared at Janice.

"If you don't know, we're certainly not going to tell you." Janice sneered, and Polly, sitting beside her, looked important and self-righteous.

Claudia felt that she couldn't even breathe, she was so mad, but at the same moment, she felt something even worse than not being able to breathe. She felt the rope loosen around her waist, and her trousers start creeping down her legs. Quickly she snapped her elbows against her waist to catch them, but the weight of the pillow inside the trousers carried them down like an express train and she had to lunge for the tops of the trousers, grabbing them just as they slid into view at the bottom of her jacket. Her face scarlet, she hiked them up and looked around. Her whole army was staring at her wide-eyed, but Janice and Polly both had their mouths in their hands and were convulsed with choking giggles.

"Come on, everybody," said Claudia. "We're going."

"Oh, must you?" asked Janice, squealing with laughter.

"It's time for Claudia and her little baby friends to go home to bed," simpered Polly. This remark was followed by more choking laughter.

Claudia opened the front door, ushered Duffy, Leonie, Maurice, Robin, and Robby out and then turned and addressed Janice and Polly. "Thank you for a lovely time," she said in her most charming, tea-party tone of voice, "you two horsey petunias!"

The laughter in the living room stopped, to be followed by a stunned silence. Claudia quietly walked out and closed the door, but not before she heard Janice say, "What kind of nasty language was that! Mo-o-o-o-o-other!"

Outside the Irby's house, Maurice asked, "What was that you said, Claudia?"

"Nothing," Claudia told him.

"It's something I made up," Duffy said. "It doesn't mean anything."

Half a block later Maurice spoke again. "That girl is all right. She makes good cookies."

"I think they're creeps," said Duffy. "I mean the girls. But Maurice is right, though, Claudia, those were good cookies."

Leonie quietly took Claudia's hand. "I hated the cookies," she said.

Claudia squeezed her hand.

After that, she wished they would go on talking and leave her out. It was too difficult to talk while she was holding Leonie's hand with one hand, holding on to her trousers and the paper sack with the other, and trying to think over what had happened, all at the same time. And she was beginning to feel sick and miserable over what Janice and Polly would be reporting to the class in the morning.

Anyway, she stopped talking and soon they all stopped talking because they were getting tired, and they all marched home in silence.

Fourteen

CLAUDIA didn't discover what news Janice and Polly had spread around the class the next morning because she never made it to the classroom.

She had long since stopped coming into the school building by the main entrance or even any of the side entrances used by the sixth grade, but had begun to go around to the back of the building to an entrance hardly used at all by the upper grades and which was off limits to the lower grades. It had a tall, prickly juniper on one side and on the other a stairwell going down to the basement heating plant. A safety patrol boy in a white chest band usually stood there to keep the little kids from using the stairs going up, or from falling down the basement stairwell if one of them wandered around there by mistake. The basement stairwell was dirty and dark, and held the collected smells of hundreds of leftover lunch remains that kids were always throwing down there when the safety patrol wasn't around. Claudia never liked to look down when she passed.

She wouldn't have looked down that morning except that she heard a queer scratching, scuffling sound from somewhere at the bottom of the stairwell. It was an animal kind of sound, as if a dog's nose was ferreting the oily remains of a tuna sandwich or a potato chip from a paper sack. Claudia thought it was probably just a dog, but she went and looked over the railing, anyway. It could have been a couple of little kids playing around down there because there was no safety patrol boy in sight.

There *were* two small kids down there, at least they seemed small at first glance. Claudia wasted no time in running down toward them. They were probably first-graders, she told herself, and she wouldn't have to do much but look at them and they would run off like scared rabbits.

But she had run only halfway down the basement stairwell when she realized that it wasn't two first-graders down there at all. There were two boys, and they were much bigger than first-graders, at least one of them was — the one who was sitting on top of the other one. His big blond head and his thick neck told Claudia at once that this was Bobby Paine.

Bobby was sitting on a smaller boy, bouncing up and down as if he were trying to push out the boy's insides. Claudia couldn't see who the smaller boy was, but lying at her feet was a pair of metal-rimmed glasses, twisted half way around, with one lens smashed. Claudia had never seen round, skinny glasses like that on anyone but Itty Bitty. This was Itty with Bobby Paine on top of him.

Each time Bobby sat down on Itty's stomach, Itty let out a soft groaning sigh. He wasn't crying or saying anything, just lying there making terrible sounds. Bobby wasn't saying anything, either. He just kept bouncing up and down.

Claudia looked wildly around for help. Where was that safety patrol boy? Where was *anyone?* The place was deserted except for the three of them. Claudia's brain spun and her stomach felt as if it were going to fall right out on the steps. She was as scared as she had ever been in her life.

If Itty wasn't getting killed, he was getting close to it, and there wasn't anyone in a whole world full of people to help him. Except Claudia. There was no one around but Claudia. And by the time she ran for help, Itty might be smashed to a pulp. That left one thing to do.

Claudia swallowed hard and took a deep breath. It didn't help much but it was the only courage she could give herself. Then she spilled down the steps and dove on top of Bobby.

Claudia's sudden arrival was a total surprise to Bobby. He lost his hold on Itty and rolled over on the cement, Claudia still clinging to him. "You let go of him, Bobby Paine! You quit it!" Claudia said in Bobby's ear.

Bobby rolled his large head around and stared at her. Then he raised his arm and gave her a grinding shove toward the wall. "What are you doing here? You keep your stupid little nose out of this! It's none of your crummy business!" Bobby's face turned such a dark red it was almost maroon.

Without replying, Claudia jumped back at him again. Her head had hit against the wall when Bobby pushed her and it hurt, not so very much, but since she was on the point of tears anyway because of the night before, because of everything, she began to cry. With tears streaming down her face, she hit Bobby. And hit him and hit him. She was sobbing and her nose dripped but she kept on hitting.

After sitting for a moment, mad but almost too surprised to do anything, Bobby quickly hoisted himself on his rear end and moved away from Claudia and Itty over to the wall, where he backed himself to a standing position. Claudia jumped up and faced him. Then Bobby started to hit her.

But he wasn't just hitting. He was trying to bite, and Claudia could feel his nails against her arms where he was clawing and scratching. Holy tomato! Bobby was fighting like a girl! That big, custard-pie bully was fighting like a girl.

What was left of Claudia's cold, scared feeling disappeared in a burning wave of anger and with it the tears and the sobbing. She was nothing anymore but plain mad. Taking a deep breath and licking up over her lip where her nose had dripped, she started pummelling Bobby again.

The fight was unequal even though Bobby fought like a disconnected windmill, his huge arms flailing in every direction. He had started kicking, too, with his big, size-eight shoes. Claudia knew that the only way she could come through the fight in one piece was for someone to show up, just anyone.

Suddenly she realized that someone was at her side hitting Bobby too. With a flashing side-glance, she saw that it was Itty, and old Itty was hitting away at Bobby like a mad rooster. Claudia stepped back a moment to get her breath, but Itty kept right on, darting around Bobby's kicking feet and neatly ducking his wild arms.

And then Bobby started to blubber. "You cut it out! You just cut it out! It's no fair. You just cut it out or I'm going to report you!" His face squeezed itself up into rubbery red lumps and he was actually crying. It was truly amazing! Blind little old Itty Bitty was beating up on Bobby and making him cry.

Claudia stood staring stupidly at them and then, happening to look up the stairwell, saw that someone else was staring at them too, and may well have been for some time — Jack Sherwood wearing the crossed straps of a safety patrol boy. At last he seemed to come to life and shouted to them, "Look, you guys, stop it! I'll have to report all of you!" Claudia wondered how much he had seen, probably a great deal from the funny look on his face.

The next thing she knew, the three of them — Bobby, Itty, and herself — were standing in front of Mrs. Marshall, the principal. Claudia looked like a female chimney sweep, her blouse torn where Bobby had clawed her, and all of her a greasy, sooty black. Her hands were bruised and scratched and her face felt as if it was too. Itty looked as bad, like some kind of comic-strip bird with his glasses, which he had tried to straighten before putting back on, hanging awkwardly on his nose as he peered through the one unmashed lens. Bobby was the only one who looked fairly tidy.

Mrs. Marshall reviewed them wordlessly for a few moments. The ticking of the clock on the wall sounded heavy and ominous, as they waited for her to say something. Bobby couldn't stand this and tears ran down his cheeks again as he made loud, wet, sniffling noises. "They started it!" he burst out finally in a sobbing whine.

The corners of Mrs. Marshall's mouth rose a fraction as she continued to look at all three of them. "So I *see!*" she said. "The thing is that I am not really interested in who started anything. I simply don't want this to happen again. I hope I'm making myself clear." They all nodded, Bobby sniffling noisily. "Now, you boys go and wash up and return to your classroom. Claudia, I think you had better run home and change your clothes after I've called to make sure someone is there. As a matter of fact, I think I should tell you that I expect to telephone all your families. Now, that is all and you are dismissed." They trailed out to the hall.

Claudia was glad she could go home first before returning to class. She almost felt sorry for Bobby because a lot of people had seen them going to Mrs. Marshall's office and the story would be all over the place. And Jack Sherwood had actually seen what had happened.

As for Itty, Claudia turned toward him as they left Mrs. Marshall's office and they exchanged glorious grins. Even with his twisted glasses and dirty face, Itty looked heroic.

When Claudia returned home, she wondered if it wouldn't have been better to have stayed and faced the class after all. Her mother was talking on the telephone when she walked in the door, stopping only long enough when Claudia appeared to inform her that she was to go up and change into something decent and then wait in her room until her mother called her. Her mother sounded far from friendly.

Claudia knew that her mother was talking to someone on the telephone about her. Was it Mrs. Marshall again? Claudia dawdled on the stairs, straining her ears. Her mother was unfairly trying to keep her voice low, but she was so agitated that it rose anyway.

"Yes, yes, Dr. Bauman . . ." (So that's who it was!) "But Dr. Bauman, she's *eleven years old!*" (So what? thought Claudia. What did being eleven years old have to do with anything? Was it a new kind of disease?) "But Dr. Bauman, she is a *girl!*" (Gee whiz! Was her mother just finding that out?) "Well, she's changing her clothes right now. We'll be over by ten. And thank you so much for seeing us, Dr. Bauman."

Claudia ran up the stairs, peeling off her clothes as she went.

Claudia loved Dr. Bauman. He was a craggy-looking man with a thick thatch of gray hair, a sandpapery face, and twinkling blue eyes, and he had taken care of Claudia for almost as long as she could remember. He always seemed to know more about her than her own parents.

While Claudia took off her clothes in Dr. Bauman's office, Mrs. Harper sat to one side in the "parent's" chair with a worried expression that made Claudia wonder if she expected to see something extraordinary. Did you break out in warts when you were an eleven-year-old girl, for heaven's sake? Dr. Bauman just sat and fiddled around with papers on his desk, which he always did when children were taking off their clothes.

When Claudia had at last peeled off her undershirt (Barbara had once remarked that Claudia would probably *never* be wearing anything but an undershirt and Claudia had said that she hoped Barbara was right), she told Dr. Bauman that she was ready.

After she was weighed and measured, she hopped up on the table and lay down. While Dr. Bauman was looking into her mouth and her ears and poking around her head, he asked her what happened at school. Claudia told him.

"Hmmm," said Dr. Bauman, trying out her arms to see if they still bent in the same place, "it seems to me that there are too many people in this world who just can't be bothered to help out their fellow man . . . don't want to get involved. Now, it appears to me that what you did was a very fine thing, young lady. And as long as you didn't get smashed to ribbons doing it, well . . ." He was looking at Claudia but she was sure he was really talking to her mother. Mrs. Harper sighed, but Claudia giggled convulsively because Dr. Bauman had started poking her stomach. She always wondered how old you were supposed to be before you were required to stop giggling when your stomach was poked. Perhaps there was a time when it stopped tickling so much. In any event, eleven years old was not that time.

"All right, Claudia, throw your clothes back on," said Dr. Bauman. While Claudia dressed, he sat down at his desk, opened the drawer and pulled out a green lollipop which he twirled in his fingers as he talked.

"Mrs. Harper," he said, "Claudia is absolutely fine physically and I don't believe there are any other things wrong, either, as you suggested. Now, there is something I'm going to say to you that I told you many years ago. It bears repeating. This has to do with some anxieties you were having about Claudia at that time. I promised you that by the time Claudia was in kindergarten she would undoubtedly *not* be carrying a baby bottle in her lunch box nor would she be wearing diapers to school." Claudia smiled at this and so did her mother. "Well," Dr. Bauman continued, "I think you understand what I'm trying to say, Mrs. Harper. Claudia will be all right. She is a young lady who manages her problems very well."

"Thank you, Dr. Bauman," said Mrs. Harper, rising to go. She still looked worried. "You don't think she needs extra vitamins or anything like that?"

"No, I don't think so at all. And say, Claudia, how's Duffy these days?" Duffy was Dr. Bauman's patient too.

"Oh, he's fine," Claudia said, looking hopefully at her mother. All she got back was an impatient, ready-to-go look.

Dr. Bauman rose and, grinning at Claudia, handed her the lollipop. "You too old for this?" he asked. Claudia reached for it. Dr. Bauman always remembered that green was her very favorite flavor.

"Of course," Dr. Bauman continued, "it will make

all your teeth rot out." He picked up the telephone which had been ringing for about fifteen seconds. "But maybe that's not such a bad thing. Give your mother something worth*while* to worry about." He winked at Claudia as they left.

The doctor's visit didn't really accomplish much, but it made Claudia feel better. Dr. Bauman always made her feel better one way or another. Her mother, however, still looked worried.

Nothing seemed much different at school when Claudia returned. Bobby Paine was sitting at his desk when Claudia walked in the classroom and he carefully kept his nose buried in the pages of a history book. Itty smiled broadly and openly at Claudia. A few people stared and one or two nudged each other. Janice and Polly first snickered and then ignored Claudia entirely. And that was all. Until art class.

Mr. Dalroy's assignment that day was for each person to draw a portrait of someone else, preferably someone that sat close-by so there would be a minimum amount of desk-shifting. In this assignment, two people usually did each other, taking turns posing. Claudia knew that no one around her would want to draw her picture, but she herself decided that she would do Polly McKisson, who had turned to face Janice. If the picture was bad enough, and she would make sure that it was, she would add it to her poison papers at home.

As they drew, Polly soon became aware of the fact

that Claudia was drawing her, and she began to squirm uncomfortably, trying to turn her face so that Janice could still see it but Claudia couldn't. Claudia managed anyway. She managed so well that she surprised herself by ending up with one of the best pieces of work she had ever done in art class. It was not very flattering, but it was a good portrait of Polly, and Claudia's was one of the few pictures chosen by Mr. Dalroy to be put on the blackboard. Claudia could tell that Sarah was staring at it.

"And now," Mr. Dalroy said at the end of the period, "I promised that I would announce the names of those I have selected to work on the Christmas show. I've decided to take one boy and one girl from each class, asking each of them in turn to choose a partner. These four along with the students from the other sixth-grade classes, will be working closely with me on designing and painting the sets. Now from this room I am going to ask . . ." He looked slowly over the room. "I am going to ask Sarah Carvell and Jack Sherwood. Sarah and Jack, perhaps you two would like to confer with each other before you make your choices. Why don't you go to the back of the room and talk it over for a minute or two?"

Sarah and Jack, with embarrassed smiles on their faces, got up and walked to the back window where they held a short whispered conference. While this was going on, Claudia watched both Janice and Polly, who had never even looked at Sarah before, nearly wiggle out of their seats trying to turn and catch Sarah's eye.

It was no wonder. Here was an opportunity not only to work with Mr. Dalroy, but Jack Sherwood as well, one of the most popular boys in sixth grade. Janice and Polly looked as if they were losing their minds over it.

The conference over, Sarah and Jack returned to their desks and Jack held up his hand. "We're ready now, sir," he said.

"Well?" inquired Mr. Dalroy.

The classroom was as quiet as the inside of a pyramid. Everyone seemed to have stopped breathing.

"We'd like Claudia Harper and Conrad Bitty to work with us, sir," Jack said.

"A fine selection," returned Mr. Dalroy, smiling at both Claudia and Itty. "I'll notify all four of you shortly on the time and date of a special meeting that we'll have to discuss our ideas for the Christmas show."

Claudia felt herself blushing up to her hair roots. She knew that all the class was looking at her.

Mr. Dalroy picked up his books and then, just as he was leaving the classroom, he turned to them and said, "Oh, by the way, I almost forgot. Do you all remember the art supplies that were missing several weeks ago?"

Everyone in the class nodded but, in addition, Claudia saw several people turn and look at her with strange expressions on their faces.

"Well," Mr. Dalroy continued, "it seems that a rat has been building his nest behind the art room walls and we've uncovered a wealth of missing things back there. Among them were the art supplies . . . and even my watch. I must have laid the watch down on a rag and forgotten it. When the rat pulled off the rag, he pulled my watch with it. So I'm happy to report that that is one mystery solved and one rat properly disposed of. I want to thank all of you who have co-operated by helping to look for these things."

When they filed out for lunch that day, several girls smiled at Claudia. They were sheepish smiles but, nevertheless, smiles. Claudia could hardly believe it. Alice Clay sidled up to her almost as soon as they reached the cafeteria. "I never believed you took those things, anyway," she said. Then she took Claudia's arm as if they had been chums for years. "If you need anyone extra for the Christmas show, I'd be glad to help."

Claudia couldn't quite take all this in at once. She had been accused of stealing! But how could anyone have believed such a story? She shook her head as if to clear it, and then looked around the room for Sarah. Sarah was not part of the group near her, but had already gone off and sat down at a table. Sarah was looking at her, almost defiantly.

"Excuse me, please," Claudia said, peeling Alice's clinging arm from her own. She strode over and took an empty place beside Sarah, dropping herself and her lunch box down with noisy thumps.

Sarah said nothing for a moment. Then, "I'm not having wheat germ anymore," she said, directing her remark to the wrapping around her peanut-butter sandwich.

"That's good," said Claudia, addressing her own lunch. They seemed to be having a conversation with their peanut-butter sandwiches rather than each other.

"You didn't have to sit with me," Sarah said.

"Didn't you want me to?"

Sarah thoughtfully sucked a blob of peanut butter off her thumb. "Yes."

"You and Jack didn't have to choose me for the Christmas show either."

"Nobody held guns to our gizzards," said Sarah.

This sounded so much like Duffy that Claudia had to giggle. It was exactly something that Duffy would say.

"Is your peanut butter the sticky kind like mine?" she asked.

"Well, all I can say is it's a good thing I'm not wearing false teeth," replied Sarah, turning to Claudia with her eyes crossed and her mouth pickle-juiced into a small circle. Claudia exploded.

The girls chewed silently and reflectively on their sticky peanut-butter sandwiches for a few moments. Then Claudia drew a deep breath and said, "What was it Janice and Polly were telling everyone about me?"

"Oh, *that*," replied Sarah. "Those dumb girls! They said you stole Mr. Dalroy's art supplies. Maybe even his watch. Boy, are they dumb!"

"Did you think I did?" Claudia asked.

"No!" Sarah exclaimed. "Half the class didn't, either. It's just that . . . you know . . . you can't fight city hall." Sarah helped herself to a stalk of celery.

"Anyway, they said you stole something of theirs but they wouldn't even say what. Who'd believe a stupid thing like that?"

"I did take something, I guess," Claudia said.

"Well, what?"

"A note. It was a note from Janice to Polly. I shouldn't have taken it, I guess. I was going to give it back but they never talked to me after that."

"What was the note about?"

"Just a dumb thing about Mr. Dalroy. A big heart with initials and all that stuff. They're in love with Mr. Dalroy."

"Is that all?" said Sarah with disgust. "*Every*one's in love with *him*." She allowed a respectable amount of silence to pass. "Are you?"

Claudia gave her an amazed stare and then made a gagging sound into her napkin.

"Good," said Sarah matter-of-factly. "I'm not, either. He's a good art teacher, though. It'll be fun working on the Christmas show."

"Did you like my picture of Polly?" Claudia asked.

"It was good. I mean your work was good. The *picture* was terrible!" Sarah grinned at Claudia.

"Hey, I'll tell you what," Claudia said suddenly. "Let's go out and throw some balls."

"I can't catch balls even if they hit me in the head," Sarah said. "About all I can do is draw and ride a horse, nothing else."

Claudia suddenly stopped chewing. "You ride *horses?*"

"I don't ride giraffes," said Sarah. "I have a horse." She said this as calmly as if everyone in the whole world had a horse every day for breakfast.

"A *real* horse?" asked Claudia, who had almost stopped breathing.

"I have it at my grandmother's in the country. Would you like to come out sometime? You can ride him."

Claudia sighed. "I don't know how."

"I'll teach you," said Sarah. "It's easy. Look, you teach me to catch balls . . . I'll teach you to ride a horse. Okay?"

"Okay!"

"There's a problem, though," Sarah continued. "What if I never learn to catch balls?"

"What if I never learn to ride a horse?"

"That doesn't bother me," said Sarah.

"Well, I don't care if you never catch a ball the rest of your life!" said Claudia, and meaning it.

"You wouldn't want to choose me for a team or anything if I can't catch."

"I don't choose people because they can catch balls," said Claudia with her nose in the air. "Duffy couldn't catch the *world* if you threw it at him."

"Who's Duffy?"

"He's my friend. He's a terrible catcher."

"Oh," said Sarah.

Fifteen

CLAUDIA flew home from school that day, wings on her heels, wings on her shoulders, everywhere wings, wings, wings! Autumn crackled all around her and the wind stung her cheeks. She flew home in it like a wild bird, feeling as if she had been touched by a magic wand. Suddenly and wonderfully she wasn't the class creep anymore and she had Sarah-who-was-a-girl-and-was-like-Duffy-and-was-going-to-be-her-friend. And she had a nice mother who worried about her, and a nice father who knew that everything would blow over and it usually did, and a sister who wasn't *too* bad, and David who was going to be home any minute, and Dr. Bauman who remembered to give her green lollipops, and a lovely room with David's old furniture in it just as he had had it and which would never get changed

171

or anything. Even if Claudia hadn't been running, she would have been breathless just *thinking* about all this.

The first thing Claudia did when she got home was race out to the kitchen to tell her mother about Sarah and being chosen to work on the Christmas show and a dozen other things. She was spilling over with things to tell about.

But the kitchen was empty. There wasn't even anything cooking on top of the stove.

"Mother! Mother!" Claudia called, running to the living room. Her mother wasn't there, either.

Finally, at the foot of the stairs, Claudia caught a strong smell of paint which she had been too excited to notice before. "Mother!" she called again, racing up the stairs.

"In here, dear," Mrs. Harper's voice was coming from Claudia's room.

Claudia galloped down the hall and burst into her room, almost falling over her mother, who was sitting on the floor on a pile of newspapers. She was wearing shorts, Claudia's old paint-spattered shirt, and had her hair done up in a huge pink bandana.

And there was paint everywhere, pink paint going on everything. Mrs. Harper was putting pink paint on Claudia's furniture — her beloved chest and bed and bookcase and no, she hadn't reached the desk yet, but that was the *only* thing that wasn't covered in pink paint.

Claudia stood still for a moment, too numb even to move. She was only vaguely aware of her mother sitting and looking up hopefully like a cat who has just laid a dead mouse at someone's feet and is waiting for praise.

Suddenly Claudia wanted to scream. She wanted to scream until the top of her head blew off. She felt as if she could go on screaming the rest of her life. It was just too horrible.

"Mummy, why?" she sobbed. Claudia hadn't called her mother "Mummy" in years. "Why did you paint my furniture?"

"Don't you like it, dear? I thought you'd like it."

"I hate it! I hate it! It isn't my furniture anymore when it's pink. It isn't David's. It isn't anybody's. It's just pink furniture. It . . . it . . . belongs to the *paint!*"

"But, Claudia," Mrs. Harper said, her voice becoming stiff, "isn't it high time you had a room that looked like a *girl's* room?"

"It *was* a girl's room! It was *my* room and I'm a girl and Dr. Bauman *said* I was all right and you didn't have to go and paint everything *pink!*" Tears ran down Claudia's chin, and she reached up and wiped her nose on her jacket sleeve.

"I haven't quite painted everything yet," said her mother, a little defensively.

"Well, you'd better not," Claudia shouted with a broken sob. "If you do, I'll . . . I'll *kill* you!" It was

173

a terrible thing to say. It was the worst thing Claudia had ever said in her whole life and she didn't mean it at all. It just came out and surprised her to pieces. Her mother looked at her as if she had already been killed. It was awful.

"All right, dear," her mother said very quietly. "If you really don't want me to, I won't. And I'm sorry for what I've already done."

That made Claudia feel worse than ever. It would have been much easier to have her mother screaming at her or even spanking her. What she wanted to do now was to throw her arms around her mother's neck and give her the biggest hug she had ever given anyone, but she couldn't. Some frightening thing inside her just kept her standing there and staring, doing nothing.

At last she said simply, "I guess I'll go out for a while."

"Where are you going?"

"I don't know. Just out."

Her mother pulled off her bandana and started to pick up the newspapers on the floor. She wasn't doing it angrily. She was just picking them up. "Well, don't be late for dinner, dear." She sounded very tired.

Hurting inside because she hated it when her mother sounded that way, Claudia turned and went slowly down the stairs.

Claudia had walked aimlessly for two blocks before she remembered that it was Friday and she was due to pick up Rosa's check at the dime store. Even with all the bad things that had happened the past few weeks, Claudia had not missed a Friday. She felt she couldn't miss that day even though she knew her eyes were a mess. Rosa counted on her, and Mrs. Olivetti counted on her to watch the children while she went to the store. When someone is counting on you in that way, you can't let a small thing like red around the eyes keep you away.

As it turned out, Rosa didn't even notice how Claudia's eyes looked. She looked herself as if she had a problem inside her head far greater than anything that had happened to Claudia. In a week she seemed to have grown ten years older. Her face was a worried white smudge against her dark hair and the chords stood out in her neck. And she seemed to have shrunk so much that she hardly filled the space of a counter stool. It scared Claudia.

"Look, honey," Rosa said, without her usual smile, "the baby's sick. He's real sick, honey. I've been worried about it all day. I thought I'd get off and go home, but they're shorthanded here and I knew you were coming. Look, honey, what I'm going to do is this. I'm going to call a cab from here and send it over to the house in about fifteen minutes. You go on home and tell Momma to get herself and the baby ready and go to this address." She pulled a paper napkin out of the holder and wrote something on it. "Tell Momma this is the clinic. Tell her I said to take the baby in the taxi and go there. Tell her to wait there until they see the baby. Tell her as soon as I get off work, I'll meet her there. She can use my pay money for the taxi. Okay? Now look, honey, you'll have a hard time telling Momma all this, but will you try?"

"Sure, I can do it," Claudia said, not really sure at all, but trying to hide it.

"Now, honey, the only thing is we might be late. It might be only an hour or so but we might be late. I don't know. Sometimes you have to wait a long time in the clinic. Can you manage the kids?"

"Oh, sure," Claudia said. She really meant that. She could manage the children all right.

"And look," Rosa said, "do you want to call your mother or something so's she'll know you're okay?"

"No, I don't need to. She knows where I am." It was a downright lie, but how could she tell Rosa that her family didn't even know the Olivettis existed? How would you explain a thing like that? Besides, she couldn't call now, anyway. Her throat still felt tight when she thought about what she had said to her mother. How could you calmly call your mother and say you would be late for dinner when you had just said that you might kill her? It was a terrible predicament.

The baby looked weird, shriveled and green like a gnome. Claudia could hardly tell that it was alive, although she knew it must be because Mrs. Olivetti was rocking it in their old rocker. The room was filled with the labored groans the rocker made as she rolled it slowly back and forth.

Mrs. Olivetti had been crying too. And as Rosa had said, Claudia did have trouble explaining what she was to do. At last, however, the message sank into her confused brain and, kissing the other three children as if she might never see them again, she rode off with the baby in the taxicab.

Claudia read to the children until she was hoarse. The electric clock in the kitchen, the one with half the enamel worn off it, quietly announced the arrival and departure of five o'clock. Claudia really began to worry about what her mother would think, but there wasn't much she could do about it. There was no telephone and she couldn't leave the children.

Six o'clock came and the children began to beg for their dinner. Claudia was not much of a cook. Fudge, English toffee, and toast were the sum total of her accomplishments in the kitchen. And sometimes she had been allowed to pour the waffle batter that her mother made onto the griddle. That was about all. She didn't think that fudge and English toffee were a very good idea for a child's dinner and she didn't remember what the recipes were, anyway. The thought of making a waffle from the beginning all by herself was ridiculous. That left toast. And maybe soup. She could open a can — she thought.

The inside of the Olivetti refrigerator was depressing, empty and forlorn, but it did at least contain a half loaf of bread and some margarine. And Claudia had no trouble finding two tins of soup in the cupboard. They happened to be minestrone which was good because that wasn't as hard to mix as cream soup. Unfortunately, the Olivetti can opener was the kind you had to bang in and then rock around. Claudia didn't hold the soup tin tightly enough and the top part of the soup, which had some grease on it, sloshed out and all over her new plaid skirt.

As she reached for the jagged lid, she cut her finger on it and then dropped the lid on the floor. The smallest child dove for it, slicing a rough gash in his hand from his wrist to his small finger. He started to scream. The two others, in nervous fright, joined him. There was blood all over the place, but Claudia finally got her own finger and the child's injured hand wrapped in pieces of clean dish towel, and had all three children seated tidily on the kitchen floor. There she served them soup and bread, bread because the toaster wasn't working.

After dinner she decided that they should have a treat and all she could think of to do was invent fudge. There was no chocolate anywhere but she did find some cocoa and with it was able, finally, to throw together a strange chocolate brew which delighted everyone, even though it never did get hard and ended up drizzling all over the place. It didn't matter. Claudia knew that children love messes and she let them lick the pan and the spoons. She had thoughtfully used three spoons to scrape the pan so each child could have a fudge spoon to chew on.

By the time Rosa and Mrs. Olivetti returned at eight o'clock, Claudia had the children cleaned up (except there was still a lot of chocolate on their faces) and in their pajamas. All Rosa could say over and over again was, "You're a doll, honey. You're a real doll." Mrs. Olivetti kept patting her on the head until she thought she'd go bald. The baby had been taken to the hospital and nobody knew yet how things would turn out with him. He was very sick, though, and Rosa was going to go down the street later and get a cab to go back to the hospital. Both she and Mrs. Olivetti looked gray from worrying.

"Oh, I'm sorry, honey," Rosa said, "I forgot all about how you're going to get home. I should have kept the cab."

"That's all right, Rosa," Claudia said. But it wasn't all right, really. It was dark out and Claudia had never in her life been allowed out alone that late, even around where she lived. Except Halloween and then she was with other children.

But she had to get home somehow and there was no use worrying Rosa and her mother any more than they already were. So Claudia ran home. She ran faster than she had ever run in her life, running so fast that her chest ached and her eyes stung, chased every inch of the way by the dark night that threatened to capture her with each step.

Too tired almost to hold herself up by the time she arrived, she still opened the door of her home quietly so she wouldn't scare anyone by bursting in. Voices reached her, coming from the living room, and she stood outside the door a moment, listening. The first voice she heard was David's. David was home! It was all she could do to keep from racing in, but the sound of his voice, the sound of all their voices held her back.

"Great Scott, Mom, the whole thing on the face of it was asinine! Painting the kid's furniture pink! Ye gods, it's enough to make a person throw up. I don't blame her for running off. I'd run off myself!"

"See here, David," Claudia's father said sharply, "there's no need for you to speak to your mother that way!"

"But David's right! Mother, Claudia adored that stuff. She positively *adored* it. You *know* she did!" That was Barbara talking and Claudia nearly fainted when she heard her. Barbara was actually sticking up for her!

"There's no use jumping on me now, any of you!" Mrs. Harper fairly shrieked at them. "I'm sorry I did it. It was stupid, I admit it. But that was no reason for her to go running off. And I don't care what any of you say, I'm going to call the police! For all we know she may be lying someplace d-d-d-dead!" She ended with a sob. Claudia's mother was crying. She was crying over Claudia's old dumb self. Claudia couldn't bear to hear it.

Creeping quietly into the living room, she said in a small voice, almost a whisper, "I'm here."

Everyone turned and faced her, frightened relief on their faces. But no one ran to her. They just stood staring.

"Where have you been, young lady?" Mr. Harper's voice was steady, but furious.

"Look, pest, you scared Mom half out of her mind," David added.

"We were going to call the *police*, Claudia. The *police!* And look at you!" Mrs. Harper's face paled with anger, but it was a scared face. Claudia knew she was talking the way she was because she was scared. Claudia looked at herself.

Her jacket was unbuttoned and that left her blouse and skirt exposed for everyone to see. And they were covered with blood and minestrone soup and fudge — great, glorious globs of Claudia's homemade fudge. She was a mess.

"All right, young lady," said her father sternly, "once again I'm asking you. Where *were* you?"

Defiance rose up in Claudia like a hot wave. They had somehow made it impossible for her to talk. She simply stood there, silent and rebellious.

"For the last time, Claudia. You will tell us where you were or you will get the spanking of your life. You may think you're too big to be whipped, but I assure you, you are not. Now, are you going to tell us!"

"Yes, I'm going to tell you!" Claudia screamed at them. "I was out at this terrible dirty place. And I was doing all the bad things there are in the whole world. I was . . . I was . . . I was SMOKING A CIGA-RETTE! And I was doing all this at Queen Street . . . 1878 Queen Street . . . and if you don't believe me,

181

you can go there and see!" She was sobbing now and nearly blinded by her tears.

"All right," said her father in a tight voice, "we *will* go and see. Your mother and I will go together and see right now. And *you* will march up to your room, and *you* will put on your pajamas, and *you* will go to bed. We will talk about this further in the morning."

Claudia ran from the living room and up the stairs to her room. She knew that she must have frightened everyone beyond belief, but why did life have to turn wonderful for all of about five minutes and then turn as bad as ever? What was it all about? Sobbing, Claudia threw herself on her bed, hiding her nose in the pillow to drown out the smell of wet paint.

It must have been about two hours later that voices in her room, voices right by her bed, awakened Claudia. Lying there with her eyes tightly shut, she listened to them whispering. The voices belonged to her mother and father.

"Imagine her going over there every week to take care of those children!" her mother said.

"Did I hear them say that she actually changed diapers?" Her father's voice went off into a surprised squeak.

"Well, I think she just did *that* once," whispered her mother. "Still, I didn't think Claudia knew whether a diaper went on a baby's head or its bottom. She really surprised me too."

Then her father said, "Couldn't we just wake her and

tell her that we took that poor woman over to the hospital and they think the baby's going to be okay?"

"Don't you dare!" breathed Claudia's mother. "She's exhausted. It can wait until morning."

"I wonder why she never told us?"

"Who knows? It's just Claudia's way, I guess. She always keeps things to herself until she works them out her own way. She always has."

"The poor kid! That poor, poor kid!" said Mr. Harper.

"I know," said Mrs. Harper with a sigh. "I could chew all that pink paint off with my own bare teeth!"

"It would be a terrible job to sand it down," Mr. Harper said, "but I'll do it if you want. Maybe she'd just accept a new color. It would be easier to paint it over."

"Well," whispered Mrs. Harper, "I think we'd better talk about it tomorrow. We really will wake her up if we continue like this."

Claudia felt her mother kissing her softly on the forehead. Then someone who had the nice smell of her father's shaving lotion kissed her after that.

As her parents tiptoed out of the room, Claudia hugged her pillow. A warm, furry feeling that started in the middle of her stomach and crept out all over her made her draw up her knees and hug them, too. This was a much nicer way to go to sleep than two hours ago when she had had trouble finding a dry place on her pillow.

And furthermore (Claudia giggled) she told herself

firmly that she would *not* (Claudia giggled again) have her mother chewing the pink paint off with her bare teeth. After all, she might even grow to like everything pink. And another thing they could do was to add some green lollipops and goofy black whales. Claudia knew that she must really be getting sleepy and silly to have thought of something like that. Imagine, green lollipops and goofy black whales all over her pink furniture! Or was it goofy black lollipops and green whales? Anyway, the last thing Claudia remembered before she dropped off to sleep was seeing hundreds of goofy little whales swimming around and around after hundreds of crazy little green lollipops. Around and around and around in a great big, huge, enormous pink sea!

Sixteen

CLAUDIA awoke the next morning with the delectable feeling that there were ten million things she wanted to do that Saturday, although when she really stopped to think about it, she couldn't name one. Probably, she thought, she would just mess around with her junk, her collections and so on, and maybe, just maybe, get rid of all her secret poison papers. Anyway, she would do things like that.

She had breakfast alone with her parents because David and Barbara were sleeping late. Her mother and father both were trying to act as if nothing at all had happened, but Claudia could tell that they were dying to talk about the night before. They were having blueberry muffins, which happened to be Claudia's favorite Saturday breakfast, and at last, as her mother was putting one on Claudia's plate, she said, "Dear, there are some things we'd like to talk to you about."

Claudia broke open the steaming muffin, drowned it in butter, and took a huge bite. She choked it down before she spoke. "Oh, it's okay. I guess I know all about last night." She began immediately to butter her next bite as if buttering blueberry muffins was the only thing in the world that mattered at that moment.

Her father cleared his throat. "You mean you . . . ah . . . were awake when we came into your room last night?"

"Sort of," replied Claudia, trying to keep the expression on her face blank. As far as she was concerned, the entire situation had been taken care of the night before, wrapped up in a small box and stored in the brain someplace where it could conveniently be removed and considered privately from time to time. Everything was resolved (except for Duffy), life was back to normal, and Claudia was in no mood for slush and goo. A conversation of this sort might become very sentimental in a hurry and somehow, in the bright light of a pleasant Saturday, Claudia didn't care to see this happen. She just wasn't up to it.

"Oh," said her mother. "Well, then, have you thought over what you might like me . . . that is . . . *us* to do about your room? Would you like to have the things sanded down or, perhaps . . . painted over?" This last suggestion was on a very hopeful note.

"Just leave it," said Claudia.

"You're quite sure," said her mother.

"Yes," said Claudia.

"Oh," said her mother.

"By the way," said her father, "sometime later this morning, if you'd like to go with us, we might just take a run down and offer to take your friend over to the hospital to see the baby. Would you like that?"

"Sure, that's okay."

"You don't sound very enthusiastic. Do you or don't you want to?"

"I *said* it was okay," said Claudia.

"Oh," said her father.

Picking up a few leftover crumbs of muffin from her plate and throwing them into her mouth, Claudia pushed herself away from the table. "May I be excused now?"

"Yes, and . . . dear . . ." Her mother hesitated.

"What?"

"Don't make any plans for tomorrow night. I think David is taking you out to dinner to that terrible pizza place you love and then to some dreadful monster movie. He asked me to remind you to save that date for him."

"Oh, boy!" squealed Claudia.

"And one more thing, we're having hot dogs for dinner tonight."

Claudia shrugged. "What about it?"

Her mother suddenly became very busy doing something at the stove. "Aren't hot dogs Duffy's favorite food?"

"Oh, sure," said Claudia.

"What your mother is trying to say, Claudia, is that we miss old Duffy around here and how about asking him if he can have dinner with us tonight?" said Claudia's father, his eyes twinkling.

This was too much for Claudia. She flew to her mother and threw her arms around her waist in an enormous hug. There was no kissing or anything, just a huge hug. "What time can he come over?" she asked suddenly.

Her mother smiled. "How about nine thirty this morning?"

"Oh, boy!" shouted Claudia, bounding out the door.

Suddenly, as if she had been tugged back by a string, she poked her head back into the kitchen. "Hey, I almost forgot. Can I invite this girl over one day next week? I mean, *may* I invite this girl?"

"What girl is that, dear?" asked her mother.

"Oh, just this girl," said Claudia. "She has a horse and everything."

"Yes, of course you may, dear. That would be just . . . just splendid!"

As Claudia ran out, she saw her mother look at her father with a helpless shrug, flop into a chair, and then stare disbelievingly after her. Now, what was wrong with her mother? Claudia wondered.

She skipped down to Duffy's house, wondering if she would see his leg dangling down from the apple tree. It was and she did.

"Holy tomato, Duffy," she called out, "are you growing there?" She scrambled over the fence.

Duffy peered through the branches and beamed at her. "Hey, are you back?"

"Oh, sure," said Claudia, climbing up beside him and immediately falling backward and hanging head down from the branch.

"What'll we play?" Duffy asked.

"I don't know. Why don't we just climb around awhile?"

"Wouldn't you like to play army or anything?"

Claudia considered this important suggestion. "No, I guess not. Hey, I have it! Let's go over and play rope with the kids." She dropped lightly down from the branch, Duffy after her.

"Rope! Claudia, are you going crazy or something?"

"Yep!" Claudia said. "Crazy! Crazy! Crazy!" And she felt kind of crazy, too, as she ran to the fence. Silly crazy! Happy crazy! Crazy crazy! She was crazy because there was suddenly a whole world full of apple trees, and a whole world full of Duffys, and a whole world full of Sarahs and green lollipops and goofy black whales, and a whole world full of Davids taking her to a whole world full of terrible pizza parlors. Holy tomato, was she crazy!

Claudia and Duffy reached the fence and started to

climb over. Splinters from the rail fence scratched Claudia's legs and the wind blew her hair in her eyes, but it felt good. Leonie and Maurice, Robin and Robby all smiled and waved as the two of them appeared.

Suddenly, Maurice raised his arm and pointed upward. The eyes of the children followed the direction of his arm, and they saw directly above them a November arrow of geese going south. With mouths open and eyes wide, they listened to the silence of the birds cutting their way through the gray sky. Watching wordlessly, they saw the arrow become, at last, a pinprick at a place where as much of the world as they could see ended. And it was not until the sky was empty of everything but a few stray clouds that they picked up their ropes and began to play again.